ISTANBUL'S
SECRET WARRIORS

* * * * *

by Jonathan P. Slow

2014

ALSO BY JONATHAN P. SLOW

COMPANION SERIES-
BIBLICAL FIGURES:
I, Joseph Father of Jesus. 2012. Amazon

I, Mary, Mother of Jesus. 2013. Amazon

COMPANION SERIES-
EXPLOITS of the SEXIEST DETECTIVE:
The Sexiest Detective in West Florida. 2013, Amazon

The Sexiest Detective in Key West. 2013, Amazon

The Sexiest Detective in Ireland. 2013, Amazon

PSYCHOLOGICAL ANALYSIS:
A Desirable Killing and the Paranoid Mind. 2013, Amazon

CROSS-CULTURAL:
Beware the Beneficent Gringo! 2013, Amazon

COMPANION SERIES-
SPY STORIES:
Istanbul's Silent Witness. 2014, Amazon

Istanbul's Secret Warriors. 2014, Amazon

Jonathan Padraig Slow, Exposed. 2014, Amazon

ISTANBUL'S
SECRET WARRIORS

by Jonathan P. Slow

Volume Two

Cover picture by Shutterstock.com

Cover by Bear

Best

SPY NOVEL

The

FLORIDA
MYSTERY WRITERS

2014

ISTANBUL'S
SECRET WARRIORS

by Jonathan P. Slow

It was the time when we Americans were surrounded by an outbreak of Arab nationalism. The British were being driven out of their former bases in colonial territories in the Middle East. Friendly rulers were being dethroned and replaced with popular leaders. The people's voices could no longer be ignored; they were taking back their countries and American interests be damned!

Never before had the Middle East been so dangerous for foreign agents. Super spy Adam Chelabi runs the whole Middle East section of the CIA from his station in Istanbul, Turkey. He is expected to know everything that is going on, and to redirect outcomes to the American advantage.

Adam used to work for the CIA Investigative branch in Paris but he suddenly found himself administering the whole CIA program for the Middle East. He is the disgruntled boss of other agents scattered throughout the region.

Although he was born in Turkey he grew up in the US. He is a former police detective, chosen for special training by the FBI and the CIA. In a previous volume of this series (*Istanbul's Silent Witness*) he takes you through the dark, tangled streets of Istanbul and, well-lit venues of cabarets that attract tourists.

Once again he teams up with Detective Abdullah of the International Istanbul Police. Join two of **Istanbul's Secret Warriors** as their adventures take them throughout the mysterious Middle East.

TABLE OF CONTENTS

SUDDEN DEATH

Istanbul Airport. 1955

SHIT!

I'm sorry to start off my narrative with such an obscene explicative but you could hardly expect a spy like me to use a mealy-mouthed expression like, "Oh my Goodness!" There's crudeness in all men's character, and I certainly am no exception.

I was just getting adjusted to the idea of going back to work after a two-month holiday. The raucous alarm in the corridor chimed in with all the other noisy devices in the Attaturk airport in Istanbul, Turkey. I sensed that somehow I was screwed, rather than knew it. Like everybody else I stood still in my tracks and didn't know what to do.

I looked around and saw jumbles of us marionettes with our strings severed. We waited for the tugs that would bring us back to life-- we waited but they didn't come.

The screaming of the alarms was replaced gradually by the cacophony of people. The ramp and lobby of the airport were filled with swiveling heads, with mouths flapping open-- all seeking an answer as to what was happening. Airport employees were no better informed than we were. As employees, they felt the obligation to assist the passengers. They looked around desperately for someone to tell them what they should do. The employees were more panicky than the passengers.

The puppeteer's voice came over the PA system, "Do not be alarmed. The airport has been shutdown for your safety. All flights have been grounded for security reasons. Please go back quietly to your departure gates and sit in the waiting areas until you are given further instructions. You are not in danger. Repeat: You are not in danger!"

I was frustrated like everyone else. It wasn't so much that we were anxious to get to our destinations, as it was to move on with our lives. I was in no hurry to leave my beloved Istanbul and join the "suits" at the US Embassy in Paris. I had no tender lips waiting for me at the arrival gate in Paris. It was just my destiny to go back to work, and so I wanted to get on with it.

Some of you have read my account of the investigation of the fire in my father's Istanbul hotel: *Istanbul's Silent Witness*, 2014 Amazon. In that case we don't need to be introduced.

I am Adam Chelabi and I work for the CIA. I just finished my two-month's leave and was on my way back to the Paris Regional Office of the CIA. My religious beliefs were founded in Islam but after 20 years in the United States I had adapted well to the Western, Christian culture.

The CIA is in the spy business and normally doesn't have specialized personnel trained in investigative methods. The FBI is not supposed to be operating in the international theater so that leaves us. My group of specialized agents is the only one trained to do international investigations in Europe and the Middle East.

I didn't like having responsibilities for CIA dirty tricks but I had learned to live with the relatively clean pursuit of international criminals. When I was engaged in investigations I was working to see justice done but when I was executing other CIA tasks I was promoting American interests at any cost.

As Deputy Chief of Investigations I got closer to the policy makers and I hated it. I didn't realize how well off I was until six months later-- CIA Headquarters at Langley made me Division Chief over all the CIA operations in the Middle East. I would have loved to quit and operate a small bait and fishing camp on Maryland's Chesapeake Bay. I didn't like having responsibility for running spies and black ops.

But let's get back to the shutdown at Ataturk Airport in Istanbul Turkey that stranded hundreds of us passengers. Nobody knew what the nature of the emergency was or how long it would be before the airport opened again. We finally gave up all hope that services would resume and we just wanted to get back to the city to reorganize our lives.

Busses departing for Istanbul were filled, and riders were standing in the isles. That didn't look very promising. Two hours later I finally worked my way to the head of the departing taxi line and joined others going to town. Only then did we hear the news from the driver-- the American Embassy had been bombed.

I tried to get more details but the driver said that nobody had been able to get close enough to see or even ask about the damage. The driver dropped the others off at their destinations but he wouldn't go anywhere near the American Embassy. I got out and walked.

I could still smell the odor of the bomb as I approached the gawking crowd. Damaged areas of the wall were cordoned off, as was the entrance. Turkish soldiers guarded the entire accessible perimeter. I had to elbow past several walls of people to reach the entrance.

None of us in CIA are expected to carry anything more than a passport for identification. I showed my diplomatic passport to the marine at the gate and he admitted me.

One side of the building was a shambles but the other side seemed intact. The inside guard accompanied me to the Ambassador's office and I found my old friend Charlie Haight sitting at the desk. He explained that as General Consul he had taken over the embassy as *charge d'affaires* in the emergency.

His staff surrounded Charlie while lower-level personnel hung back in readiness to carry out their superior's orders. I impatiently inquired about casualties:

<u>Deceased</u>:

Morris Cohen, US Senator from NY
Harrison Houghton, American Ambassador
Helen Scroggs, Secretary to the Ambassador
Miriam, Serving girl
Warren Lucas, Chief AID (CIA Chief)
Norman Moore, Bodyguard to Warren Lucas

<u>Seriously Wounded</u>:

William Wilson, Asst. Chief AID

After expressing my sympathies I briefed Charlie on the reason for my being in Istanbul; he wasn't interested. He declared that I was being drafted to take charge of the investigation into the bombing. I was to use the apartment and office of the deceased AID Director; his bodyguard and secretary went with the job. His car and chauffeur would await my pleasure.

He directed his next order to me but wanted all staff present to witness, "Adam, you have full permission to use any and all embassy resources to investigate this bombing. We need to know who was behind it and assess the risk of more such actions from the perpetrators."

He added some excellent advice to all:

"Never play the terrorist's game in matters like this. The terrorist wants us to lose our heads and become careless. Remember: Don't pursue revenge but seek to understand what happened. Only in that way can you protect your country from adverse results and consequences. At all times consider how you can manage circumstances to the advantage of your country. Be professionals-- don't let your personal feelings determine your behavior."

I begged Charlie to excuse me for bothering him one last time and then I declared, "I would like to have my old friend Abdullah of the Istanbul International CID at my side on this one. Please order him a 'Good Until Cancelled,' unrestricted pass to the Embassy."

Charlie smiled encouragingly, "Yeah, good idea. I know Abdullah, so there's no problem." He turned to the Marine sergeant and said, "Did you get that? Can you take care of arranging it? You have my verbal authorization." The Marine saluted his assent.

The next thing I did was phone Abdullah. He answered from his car. He said he was already down at the Galata Bridge and crossing the Golden Horn that very minute. I made sure his pass would be waiting at the front gate.

I was overwhelmed like everybody else, but my training kicked in and I started to conserve evidence immediately. I took both my bodyguard and my secretary along with me to assist. I directed them to a few peripheral objects or damaged places that we needed to capture in photos.

We hesitated entering the area where the bodies were still lying. My professional explanation for delaying was that we needed to protect the evidence. At the same time I realized that I was human enough to feel reluctance over encountering the bloody messes that once were my coworkers.

I had another excuse for delaying-- I was stalling until Abdullah arrived so that we could review the crime scene together. We were a good team; we had bounced ideas back and forth before when we were investigating my father's hotel fire a year ago. We worked well together.

I got a warm feeling when I thought about seeing Abdullah again. It's funny how we don't make time for important things, like friends. We let trivia rule our lives. Then the next moment he was there-- coming toward me with arms extended. We looked more like long-lost brothers than two detectives teaming up to catch the bad guys.

We reconstructed the events surrounding the bombing as we walked together through the scene. I loved working with Abdullah. Also, I realized that I needed his undercover police assistance to explore the complicity of known resistance groups.

WHO DONE IT?

ABDULLAH and I had three ways to track down the bomber:

1. We could interrogate embassy personnel for suspects.

2. We could use informants to stumble around in resistance groups located in the Middle East.

3. We could consider particular American policies that might have provoked the attack.

The bombing shut down the American Embassy and left it without a proper ambassador. Time was of the essence. This bloody action might be only part of a larger protest. We had to move quickly to defeat any additional plans for attacking American targets in the Middle East. We had to triple our efforts and proceed simultaneously with all three phases of the investigation.

Exposing the facts promptly is very important so that your enemy won't have time to put his own twists and spin on the events. We needed to come up with explanations for the event that would preserve the public image of America and even provoke sympathy for our loss. The opposition would be hoping for the opposite-- that the attack could be made to appear as a well-deserved punishment for America.

Politicians on both sides would instinctively use the event to their advantage. Their agitation and meddling over the bombing could only bring about a rupture in the relations between our two countries. Disruptions of relations between countries should be intentional and planned, not accidental.

Americans would demand an explanation of why Turkey let these bombers kill an American ambassador and a US senator. Some journalists would even hint at possible collusion by the Turkish government. Most troublesome was that the enemy killed a much-admired supporter of Israel. Turkey had to answer to the US but the Americans had to reassure a cantankerous Israel.

* * * * *

The Turkish people generally were opposed to their government's strong pro-American support. The government was silencing protesters and filling the jails with journalists. America was trying to make a success of an unworkable arrangement-- American political interests and those of Turkey were too different to coincide.

The Baghdad Pact had just been concluded. America had flaunted its international political and economical power by bringing together quarrelsome: Turkey, Iran, Great Britain, Pakistan, and Iran. This alliance empowered national leaders, to collaborate in repressing the Arab people, and keeping them enslaved and subservient to Western interests. These countries did not make happy bedfellows, but Washington was pushing the lie that they were all great friends.

The "truth" that Russia was promoting was a different picture. Their propaganda portrayed Israel as a rogue state established by America and Britain to steal Arab land and maintain dissention. The Russians were trying to expose the Israeli strategy that kept the Arabs marginalized in every sense.

Senator Cohen was part of the con. He brought Turkey millions of dollars for public works as well as some economic support from American citizens to be distributed privately. Official and unofficial commitments promised military assistance to help repress any internal or external opposition to the arm-twisting Baghdad Pact. America insisted on projecting the picture of "One happy family."

Everything at the embassy had been organized around the visit of NY Senator Morris Cohen. His official visit was to create a public event to praise the cooperation between our two countries in the struggle against Communism. Now everything was in a shambles.

* * * * *

We started reconstructing the crime immediately while the evidence was fresh and the people involved still would remember the details. With most of the first day already gone, we had to work late on into the evening. We had a late supper with Charlie, the charge d'affaires, to put together our pieces of the puzzle and prepare and revise our strategies for proceeding with the investigation. We were able to assemble enough information to construct a plausible scenario despite many unanswered questions:

Senator Cohen arrived the previous day. He and the Ambassador dined together quietly at the embassy that evening. The next day the Ambassador arrived at his desk at the usual 9:00 A.M. and signed the paperwork from the previous day. His administrative staff joined him in his office at a special meeting to review the program of activities involving Senator Cohen.

By 10:00 A.M. the Ambassador was ready to open his door for visits from his staff, concerning matters of the day.

Later, the Ambassador retired to an alcove in the reception room to have tea by himself so he could reflect on the morning's activities and plan the remainder of the day. This was the room in which the bomb undoubtedly had been planted, but we had no idea when.

The daily security inspection was made at the beginning of the day so the bomb probably was planted there after the start of the business day. The reception room was reserved only for officially scheduled meetings so it seems likely that it still was "clean" as late as 11:00 that morning.

The Ambassador returned to his desk at about noon. At 1:00 P.M. he went back to the reception room to greet Senator Cohen for their formal meeting. Helen Scroggs, Secretary to the Ambassador, joined them.

Warren Lucas was invited to the meeting because he was the head of the Regional CIA ops and involved in security matters associated with the Baghdad Pact. He was delayed in the anteroom on an important matter.

All were assembled and getting ready to begin after refreshments were served. A male servant, Mehmet, took orders for drinks and left to prepare them in the attached kitchen.

A serving girl Miriam brought in tea and sandwiches. It was at this time, 1:10 P.M. that the bomb exploded and killed all those in the reception room.

A bodyguard had been stationed outside the door to the reception room. Standing next to him was Warren Lucas, Chief of AID, waiting to be summoned into the meeting by the Ambassador. Both were killed when the explosion caused the wall next to them to collapse and crush them. The Assistant Chief of AID (actually CIA) was badly wounded but survived to resume his job at the Embassy.

As usual, not much of the explosive device was left. Inferences about the nature of the bomb were more dependent upon the damage it did than on any physical debris form the bomb itself. The area with the most damage was where the Ambassador was seated. The ceiling on that side collapsed and showed a lot of scorching. The interior wall of the room was blown out and it buried the two victims in the anteroom room. The embassy was intact aside from this relatively small area.

Our Military Attaché looked over the blast scene and confirmed what we were thinking. The bomb probably was only about the size of one or two shoeboxes and was placed so as to target the senator and the ambassador. A careful search located some metal fragments that undoubtedly were part of the electrical trigger. The contents of the bomb tended to rule out homemade construction-- it had been purloined from, or provided by some military group. The bomb could have been stolen from a regular ordinance supply warehouse or it might have been obtained from an illicit arms dealer.

The person, who planted the bomb, was familiar with the interior layout and knew the embassy program for that day. While not large, the size of the bomb precluded anyone from openly carrying it into the room to the meeting. Our short list of possible perpetrators immediately shrank to employees who had access to the reception room that morning. We started ticking off the list:

Morris Cohen, US Senator from NY
Harrison Houghton, Ambassador
Helen Scroggs, Secretary to Ambassador
Mehmet, Barman
Miriam, Serving girl

The first two on the list could be crossed out because they would not have wanted to cause their own deaths. Helen, the secretary would make an unlikely bomber. The barman and the serving girl were killed so they seemed unlikely suspects, but somebody had to be the culprit. Perhaps one of the servants was a suicide bomber-- ready to sacrifice his own life to be sure that the targets were taken out?

Abdullah and I pulled out the personnel files. It didn't take long to exclude the Ambassador's Secretary. She was the daughter of a Congressman and lived all her life in the Washington area. She worked for the State Department for ten years in the Central Office before being posted to Turkey. She served Ambassador Houghton faithfully for the past three years. She was 100% clean.

The barman, Mehmet worked as a driver for the embassy for ten years. His trusty service record earned him a promotion to an inside job as one of the corps of domestics. He had served for four years in that capacity. He was married with children and had a clean record as a person and employee. He was a practicing Muslim and lived in the Fethiye district, a neighborhood of conservative Muslims who were seldom involved in political violence.

Abdullah reminded me that the police had numerous sources of information and he would assign one of his sergeants to contact all their undercover policemen and collaborators and in the Fethiye district. The next day Abdullah handed me a report showing that the barman had always been above reproach or suspicion.

We were down to the last person on our list of people who had the opportunity to plant the bomb in the reception room. If the servant girl Miriam, were cleared we would have to find a new direction to go. When Abdullah reported next day he shared the information from his agents that cast suspicion on Miriam.

Miriam was from a family in Anatolia that practiced the Alawi doctrine of Islam. Whirling dervish dancing is prominent in their rituals although the orthodox Muslims reject that form of worship. Miriam was faithful in her Muslim prayers and observed the month of fasting.

She was taken on as an employee at the Embassy in the belief that an Alawi like her was unlikely to be influenced by the radical Muslim religious groups. But it was becoming apparent that she did have a Turkish/Muslim social conscience after all. She had even been arrested the previous year for protesting against American interference in Turkish affairs. There was no record of her arrest that would have brought her behavior to the attention of the Embassy because she lied to the police about her name and family.

Well, a majority of Turks opposed American interference in their affairs-- hardly a basis for suspicion. But Miriam had been one of the few who could have planted the bomb. Now we were at a standstill-- we couldn't question a dead woman. Miriam was not only a promising suspect but also our only one. We dropped all else and concentrated on learning everything about her.

Abdullah and I went out to where she lived and questioned her neighbors. We explained that we were investigating the bombing because we believed that her family might be eligible for compensation by her American employer. Money is better than honey for attracting Turkish flies.

I was the big had heard We should have had the decency to let the poor woman rest in peace if she gave her life for "the cause." Whoops! I needed to reexamine my allegiances! Was I trying to solve a crime or was I justifying a heroic act of an anti-American martyr?

Miriam had passed many clearances, but perhaps they were old-- they had failed to reveal what we learned. She sent monthly remittances to the Jerusalem Army (*Jaish el-Qudz*) in occupied Palestine; beginning about the time she started working in the Embassy.

The size of the donations was not remarkable. Rather, it was the dedication behind these payments that was alarming. She was the only support for her mother and sister, living in a crowded area of Istanbul. They couldn't afford to make these remittances, yet she never missed a payment.

The radical group was known to have supported bombings by civilians. They had been actively recruiting members in Turkey and found a devoted one in Miriam. What could have turned her from a passive sympathizer into an active supporter of this group?

One of Abdullah's informers came up with something that put a whole new light on our case. Five years earlier, Miriam's father had deserted the family and run off to Palestine to aid in the resistance to Jewish occupation. The informant said that they had never heard anything about him again.

But Abdullah had a connection with an old-time member of the Jaish el-Qudz so he persisted with his inquiry. That informer told him that Miriam's father died in a suicide bombing in occupied Palestine. He died a celebrated martyr, who took more than twenty Israeli's with him. The true numbers killed are never really known because both sides lie.

So it turned out that the father of our friendly, pleasant domestic had another role in life-- as a suicide bomber! Years ago a compensatory bonus was hand-carried to the family of her martyred father. The degree of her involvement was increasingly clear.

The same source that transmitted the suicide bonus compensation made a payment of 5,000 dollars to Miriam just a week before the present bombing. We had absolutely no material evidence of her guilt but we had a growing net of circumstantial evidence.

Normally, we would have called in the suspect for questioning, but this time we couldn't do that because she was dead. Where to go next? We looked again, and closer, at her personal life. She was living in the Fethiye district with her mother and sister in a small flat. By now it was no secret in the neighborhood that the police were inquiring about her.

This lifting of the secretive approach permitted us to meet her family and question them directly on all matters of interest. Miriam's mother was shy and reluctant to speak with us. She enveloped herself in her *abayah* and answered in brief grunts. She never made eye contact so it was hard to judge when she was lying.

We looked for collaborators. Apparently, Miriam had never revealed anything about the agent who made compensatory payments to the family for her father's suicide bombing. Everybody protected everybody else. She did mention to her family that she received a big payment just a week before the present bombing, but said nothing about the courier.

When you are from a small country you can't help feeling sympathetic to others who have to defend themselves from bigger powers. Of course, both Abdullah and I remembered how it was necessary for the Turkish heroes to drive the Greek invaders out of Anatolia after WWI. Abdullah and I were OK with our failure to identify the enemy courier who would escape being arrested.

Miriam's sister was polite but not friendly. She berated us for disturbing them while they were in mourning. We made our apologies but also made it clear that we were determined to have our questions answered. The sister cursed all of us.

She explained to us that she had been married but her husband left her to go fight somewhere in the Middle East. She was in the next to the last month of pregnancy with her first child. There didn't seem to be much more she could tell us short of a confession on behalf of her sister.

Abdullah and I returned to the embassy to check to see if Miriam's behavior had been different just before the bombing. We talked with her coworkers and they were shocked that we suspected that she had something to do with the bombing. She was well-liked and never grumbled about her work or talked politics. She was regarded as a happy, friendly person with a lot to live for.

She was in the last month of pregnancy and was looking forward to the birth of her new baby. Abdullah and I reached the same conclusion-- Miriam didn't seem like a martyr on the brink of sacrifice. She would want to live to nurse and rear her newborn baby. The profile she offered just didn't fit that of a suicide bomber.

Then we did a second take! Recalling that Miriam was pregnant, we wondered that Miriam's sister would be at the same stage of pregnancy. Did they both go to the same picnic?

Whoa! We missed something! Miriam died in the bombing but there never was any mention that her fetus was also a casualty. Did it die in the bombing, too? We searched frantically through our files to find the medical examiner's report. I scanned it carefully. Miriam's body was terribly pounded but the internal organs were sufficiently intact to permit an acceptable autopsy examination.

There was no mention of a fetus! How careless! But was it careless? Perhaps the body in the morgue was not the about-to-be mother, Miriam.

But everybody thought that they knew the person killed in the bombing. If someone else had taken Miriam's place at the embassy the employees would have noticed the absence of the swollen abdomen.

But if someone did stand-in for Miriam, she would have had to fill out the abdominal area under her dress to carry out the impersonation. How convenient! She could have strapped a bomb around her waist to help her look like Miriam. That would also explain how an impersonator would be able to enter the embassy without a full body scan or adequate pat down.

At last it became clear: Miriam must have selected the senator as a target and knew when he would be meeting with the Ambassador. Then, Miriam's sister took her place at work that day.

Miriam was only a conspirator. Miriam's sister had committed the bombing and now lay in the morgue. We had been interrogating Miriam herself, not the sister. The sister was the patriot, the martyr, the criminal-- but she could not be touched by praise or punishment.

The governments would want to come down hard on Miriam but would be deterred somewhat. First, Miriam did not actually cause the bombing and secondly, all Middle Easterners would sympathize with the family for having lost another martyr in the Zionist war. The Turkish public would not tolerate the prosecution of the sister of the poor, dead martyr.

As I prepared my report I realized that the conspirators would probably get away with a slap on the wrist instead of a noose around the neck. I didn't have a problem with that, but then I'm not an Israeli.

A GRINDING HALT

THINGS couldn't get any worse but they sure weren't going to get any better. America's enemies had closed down a major embassy. They took out the liaison between Turkey and the US at a critical time. The Ambassador and the Chief of the most important CIA Division were wiped out.

Those two critical positions couldn't be filled by just anyone. We were not only in a quandary; we were at a standstill. The Secretary of State made it clear that we were to restart operations as soon as possible. There wouldn't be time to fill the vacant positions with lengthy patronage dealings. The message was clear, "Our present situation is very dangerous. Fill the jobs and get rolling as fast as you can!"

No wonder the State Department was near panic. It was only three years earlier that the determined, imperialist Western adventurers lost Egypt. The people's revolution removed a traitorous King Farouk to replace him with an Arab nationalist hero, Gamal Abdul Nasser.

As if that weren't enough, Iran's Prime Minister Mosaddegh became a major threat to the West. He was playing Soviet Russian power against the British control held through the king, Shah Pahlavi. The preliminary round had begun when Mosaddegh nationalized Iran's oil wealth just two years earlier.

In retaliation, America and Britain had unabashedly financed a successful coup d'etat against Mossadegh. The popular Mosaddegh was toppled by a minority of special interests who were in support of the Shah. The Shah had barely recovered some control when a revolution finally removed him from the throne.

At that time our biggest network of spies and collaborators was in Iran-- more than in all the Arab Middle East combined. We spent millions to spread propaganda and buy vocal advocates to promote our policies. We had Iranian student support-- they wanted Western liberalism.

Our interference in Irani politics bore bitter fruit. The Irani reaction was a public outcry against Western interference, and the citizens viewed Russia as a friend protecting them from the American enemy.

Russia was not only playing buddy with Iran but with all the other Midle Eastern countries, too. The Egyptian monarch had been deposed a year earlier. Gamal Abdel Nasser and the army took control of the country and Russia was overjoyed.

Nasser was tremendously popular, not only in Egypt but in all the Arab world. The Arabs were waiting for a leader to arise from among themselves to lead them in the recovery of the land lost to the Jewish settlers. All hopes were pinned upon Nasser.

Iraq was in ferment too. Only a few years earlier the Iraqi Kurds revolted and the army was dispatched to enforce martial law in the north. Pitched battles solved nothing and the "Kurdish Problem" remained roiling in the background. Iraq had been too long under the tight control of the pro-British prime minister, Nuri Said.

Lurking behind this was the risk of confrontation of two major military forces, US and Russia. These are just some of the particular events that concerned us and involved massive, ominous threats.

Both sides in the Cold War possessed the bomb and were threatening one another. At the same time both were siding with smaller nations and promising to protect them against the threat of being dominated by the other major power. The polite term for this policy was "Détente," but confusion and deceit became the diplomacy of the day.

* * * * *

What I was afraid would happen, did happen. The State Department advised the charge d'affares that I had been appointed Middle Eastern Regional Director of the CIA, stationed in Istanbul. My cover would be Middle East Regional Director of AID.

I enjoyed my earlier work with the CIA, aside from a few particularly unpleasant assignments. Now that I was the high-ranking CIA officer in the Istanbul office I had an uneasy feeling. I didn't want to get caught up in the clash of Goliaths that hovered over us. But my life was not my own-- I belonged to the CIA. So I just shut up and went ahead doing what had to be done.

Nobody asked me if I wanted to be a CIA administrator-- they just told me! It was a game of tag and I was "it." I didn't want to be hopping around the world like James Bond, 007, nor did I want to be one of the Washington "suits." I just wanted to be an investigator of international crimes.

I really wanted to quit my job right there and then, but "Once a spy, always a spy." I shut up and called Abdullah to see if he could meet me. I was overwhelmed and I needed a friendly face and an encouraging smile.

I felt better after we finished most of a bottle of Raku (distilled liquor). Abdullah kept telling me that I still would have options in my new Chief's job-- maybe I could even help make the world a better place because of the understanding that my background provided.

I realized that most of what he was saying was bullshit-- nothing would change the facts. I was lonely and unhappy with my life. I was forced to always work alone and even when I was off duty I really wasn't free to make friends. Now I had been elevated in rank and further isolated by two bodyguards. Thank God I had a friend like Abdullah and my wonderful family.

In times of political instability you can do one of two things-- you can wait and let things happen naturally or push things to move in the desired direction. America always seemed to choose the bullying option and ended up the loser. It was America's long-term destiny to support the dictatorial, oppressive governments abroad instead of working to promote the welfare of the people.

I had a shitty job; I kept wishing I were on the other side. I was never a Communist but I sure as hell was for the common people. In those days it was hard to be both. You either had to be a Communist or an American; you couldn't be a liberal democrat and yet be a loyal American.

Senator McCarthy had the country mesmerized with his contention that Communists had infiltrated all branches of the government. There were no longer any liberal Americans; they were skewered with the Communist designation. All of us in government were forced to toe the line. We no longer had the right to question the policies formulated by Washington. I shut up and did my work; I went ahead and did my job. I took tasks as they came and dealt with them expediently. I just tried to ignore the larger international diplomatic picture whenever possible.

SECRET PRISON

RUSSIA had been sending military supplies and food to the Middle Eastern countries for decades before I joined the CIA. They were trying their best to compete with British influence in the Central Asian Soviet republics and all the rest of the Muslim countries in the Middle East. It was a tall order but the Soviets began a major economic assistance program in Afghanistan in the 1950s. Between 1954 and 1978, Afghanistan received more than $1 billion in Soviet aid, including substantial military assistance.

The Americans decided to stick their noses in the tent flap in direct competition with Russia. In the long run, the task of subverting countries like Afghanistan to Western ways was doomed to failure, but nobody seemed to care.

Washington could have had my opinion if they wanted it, but they seldom listened to any voices other than their own. CIA policies were made at the top of the bureaucracies, as with most government agencies. They formulated the sub goals and the routes to achieve them. We were hired to carry out orders not to think about policies. When we signed on we understood that we gave up our right to make value judgements about Washington's foreign policies.

We spies were the ones who had to deal with the conflagrations that broke out in Afghanistan, while the two major powers were playing out the cold war in their comfortable offices. It was a clandestine war so both countries used surrogates and agents to do their dirty work instead of depending upon their own military.

I suppose that should make me happy because it dumped a lot of covert work on my division and made me essential. Turkey was of strategic importance geographically, as was Afghanistan. These two countries were buffer states between the Soviets and the Western controlled Middle East. I was right in the middle of it all with my office for the Middle East CIA in Istanbul.

* * * * *

My field agents reported that the Soviets were operating a secret prison somewhere in Afghanistan. Washington had accumulated reports about several Americans and some undisclosed agents disappearing there. Of course the Soviets, both Russian and Afghan, denied any knowledge of the lost persons. Permission to visit their restricted military encampments was denied. Amnesty International had no better luck. The State Department talked with Langley and they decided to place in effect the "Red Rescue" operation that had been cooked up in the State Department.

Red Rescue had a simple objective-- locate the clandestine prison and rescue at least one prisoner who could expose to the world the injustice of extra-legal Soviet imprisonments. Langley didn't care how my agents and I accomplished the mission just so long as it succeeded.

This meant that we even had a licence to kill guards, but like everything else in the operation it would have to be done quietly. This type of operation is very tricky because the enemy can reverse the outcome of the operation by causing it to fail. Then they can complain to the world of the unwarranted aggression by the Americans. I liked neither the planned operation nor the policy it was based upon.

I had been taking orders all my life-- I didn't know any other way to conduct my affairs. I had almost stopped making useless moral judgements because they no longer influenced my behavior. So when Washington told me to go out and help a prisoner escape, that's exactly what I set out to do.

While the détente with Russia may have been successful in preventing war, it kept the foreign relations pot boiling. My division was increasingly busy with matters relating to countries being denounced as communist. I was hard put to find an agent with time to help clean up ongoing operations let alone begin new ones. But I had to send someone to Afghanistan in support of the agent we had placed there earlier.

The only agent I could spare was Nicko, who was planted in the Greek section of the Mediterranean island of Cyprus. There were no new frictions between the Greek Cypriots and the Turkish ones, so I felt OK about pulling Nicko and sending him to Afghanistan. Armed truce had been in force in Cyprus for several years and was holding.

Nicko was an anomaly we hired during the outbreak of violence between Greeks and Turks in Cyprus. His knowledge of Greek as well as Turkish was very helpful for getting in close to the people. But we hadn't found much use for him outside of Cyprus. He would have loved for us to ship him off to our Paris office to help out there. Naturally, all our agents wanted to live in Paris. The long lost of applicants precluded his having the slightest chance of moving there.

Nicko could manage almost anywhere in the Middle East but he couldn't move inconspicuously because of his language deficits. He could get along in most places by speaking Turkish. When he became desperate he could call on a smattering of Urdu and Arabic.

Nicko did have one valuable asset for some assignments-- he was an electrical engineer. That was a sufficient reason to choose him to locate the secret prison. On his way to Afghanistan Nicko stopped in Istanbul for me to brief him and to collect some technical equipment.

Nicko flew into Kabul to meet his Turkish partner named Abbas. After he settled into the CIA safe house they dined together at a nearby hotel. They sat unobtrusively in a corner and were able to converse without being overheard. Nicko transmitted my instructions to Abbas and they talked about the operation in general terms. It was hard to become specific about the details when they didn't even know the location of the secret prison. For all we knew such a prison might not even exist.

The next morning they poured over maps. They marked out regions that would be ideal locations for such a detention center. There sure were a hell of a lot of them! It would have taken months to inspect all the regions so they had to shorten the list considerably. They contacted me and asked me to review the list with my staff and make suggestions. I gave them a little help, but not much.

They needed a gimmick to help them direct their efforts. Next day Abbas arranged to meet with an undercover assistant who worked in the postal system. We prompted the postal worker to ask his colleagues about Russian mail from Kabul, "Was some of it being sent regularly to an address in an isolated part of the country?"

Two regions came up as a result of their inquiry. My agents drove out to the closest one on the list and checked into a hotel. They explained their presence by saying they were authors of travel books and wanted to rest up for a few days. A likely story! But who could come up with a better one to explain their suspicious visit to such an out-of-the-way spot?

The following day the agents tried to learn why the Russian mail was being sent to this isolated spot. They became friendly with the townspeople and one of the questions they asked was, "Do you have any family working in that big, restricted area up in the mountains?" A few people even acknowledged working there themselves.

Without difficulty Abbas and Niko learned that the area contained a sanatorium for Russians with active tuberculosis. Crosschecking brought the same answer. They scratched that village off their list and moved on to the other promising region.

It took two days of overland travel to get there but it would be worth it if they could find the secret Russian detention camp. My agents checked into a hotel and nosed around quietly. This village was isolated and for good reason-- the residents were mostly foreigners, and worked in the presumed Russian detention center. It was no coincidence that there was a heavy postal communication between Kabul and this outpost. It was the Russian prison we were looking for.

My two agents set about making friends with the guards from the prison. On their days off there wasn't much to do except sit around and talk. It wasn't long before my guys had learned enough to be able to begin their operation. We found out that this center was primarily for insurgents. You could end up here if you were a prominent protester over the occupation or even if you opposed Russian policies.

There were almost 200 prisoners at that time-- most of them held only on suspicion. If there had been adequate evidence they would have been given trials and would have been sent to serve time in a regular Soviet prison.

This prison population was made up of misfits who didn't belong anywhere else. Some of them were spies in the service of the Western Allies-- those were the ones we were most interested in.

We wanted to expose the Russian violations of human rights. Accusations from a Christian, European prisoner would get better press coverage that the whining of thousands of abused Muslim peasants.

If the world learned that the escapee was one of our own agents everybody would figure that it served him right for spying. But, we decided to go ahead anyway to try to locate one of our own guys. We would have to be careful to maintain his innocent tourist cover so he would retain his propaganda value. .

Friendly American newspapers were always ready to print our carefully composed accounts. Generally they depended upon the government for press releases to fill their empty pages. Subscribers like to read these articles that detail the actions of American heroes, so the slanted releases were seldom questioned or verified.

Our agents kept up their friendly visits with locals while moving closer to selecting a prisoner to be rescued. We needed somebody to turn into a propaganda hero. The stronger the Western connections the better-- we wanted readers to identify closely with the poor victim of Russian savagery. If necessary we would rename him with a British-sounding name.

Meanwhile our agents had been developing a small group of drinking companions in town. Since our agents came to town they had become accustomed to drinking French brandy instead of cheap vodka. They needed the inflow of fresh cash. It was just a matter of choosing a guard or two from this bunch of easy prospects. They were Russians, conscripted to work in Afghanistan, not noble fighters. Any two of the guards could manage the escape of a lone prisoner.

The jailers had affixed a plaque to each cell door to provide guards with basic information needed to deal with that particular inmate. Posting such information had been short-sighted because it made our task easier. We developed a short list of prospects by selecting only Americans or those fluent in English.

During the previous year or two, a couple of agents disappeared. We preferred rescuing one of our own agents if we found one in this prison. We needed one of the guards to find out if any of the prospects on our list was a CIA agent.

Identification of a CIA agent is a bit tricky. He is not allowed to carry a union card or any job-related material. If his boss is not available then the identification is made by spoken word. Every so often, Langley issues a new code phrase and the reply that assists in identifying an agent.

The query portion at that time was "My name's Joe. What's yours?" The answer portion was, "So is mine." All we needed to do was give a guard the query portion and he could report the response back to us. We selected one of the guards and put him on the payroll. Then he said to each of the prisoners on our short list, "My name's Joe. What's yours?"

Our guard returned from duty and told us that the answer the first prisoner gave to the query was, "What are you, some kind of a nut?" The second prisoner responded with "So is mine." We had everything we needed to effect the escape except for one thing-- we needed a second guard. Our new recruit offered to get his buddy on board.

When on duty, guards stayed in residence 24 hours a day. They were rotated weekly-- one week on duty and the following week off. The second recruit removed the first guard's clothes and passed them to the escapee. Then he tied up his mate securely to make it appear that the escapee had overcome and completely disabled him. Then the escapee dressed in the guard's clothes and joined the retiring guards in the departing truck.

Identification at the main gate was superficial. The weather was always cold and everybody was bundled up against the chill. Faces were barely visible so hasty inspection on departure depended upon a gross body count. The six departing guards were accounted for and the truck drove on into town.

The next morning our second recruit raised the alarm and assisted his partner in getting loose from the rope that had disabled him all through the night hours. The escape alarm was sounded but it was too late.

My CIA agents were waiting in town to hustle the escapee into a car and drive out of town on the back roads. With a 10-hour's head start the Russians couldn't catch up. Eventually the three reached a safe house in Kabul, Afghanistan. They holed up there for a week while waiting for my arrival.

My boys had done an excellent job. I brought our prize to the Paris CIA office. The CIA and State Department personnel cooked up the best propaganda story of the year. Time magazine devoted a cover picture and a lot of space to the story. All Americans were incensed that the Russians could treat "Innocent American tourists" so barbarously.

YASSER

YOU probably think that all us spies do is run around poisoning and shooting one another. Most of our work is precautionary. We Americans keep busy assuring that the outcomes of events are favorable to the US. That's a big job because our country is trying to run the whole world and the world is usually pissed at us.

You might say that a lot of our work is running confidence games on the public. My first trip to Palestine provides a good example of the enormous con we supported for years in the Middle East. The operation involved the impersonation of a major player on the world scene.

The con started when Israel was running out of excuses for not attending peace conferences. She complained that the Arabs wouldn't negotiate in good faith-- they wouldn't accept preconditions to any talks. Israel made sure that the preconditions were unreasonable and persisted in the claim that no person or party truly represented the Palestinians. All this posturing created a stalemate so that Israel could continue to occupy Arab territory and even build more Israeli settlements there.

It was becoming impossible to pretend that Israel was sincere in seeking a mutual peace agreement. Israel was discredited internationally. This was bad for America because the rest of the world was realizing that we were insincere in our negotiating and that our word was no longer meaningful. Something had to be done.

Our State Department "suits" sat down with their counterparts in Britain and Paris and constructed a straw man. What was needed was an Arab, who would appear before the world as a man of peace-- one who could bring peace to Israel. At the same time this leader, created by the West, would have to be content to remain a puppet.

We would offer him support and protection as well as fame and pseudo-power. All he had to do was make appearances, read the script we provided him with, and nod his head once in a while so that the crowds would see him acting like a real person. We crafted a candidate named Yasser.

It took a hell of a lot of background work to subvert the will of the people and get them to let him represent them. The people were not exactly behind him but they were fed up losing every skirmish to restore their lands. A really strong leader never had emerged spontaneously. As one analyst put it, "Yasser was able to muster a little support from a bunch of tired losers, who longed desperately for someone to speak for them."

We got away with it. Opposition to Yasser was actively discouraged and even eliminated. Our sleepers infiltrated groups of dangerous protesters and fingered them to the Israelis so that they could be pulled out of the game. Mossad was everywhere plucking out resistors in order to silence them. We spent unbelievable millions buying off opposition figures and inducing others to support Yasser. By the time we got through with our political engineering we had created a head of state, who had no will of his own.

We had to be constantly alert for threats to assassinate Yasser. We used every trick in the book to keep him alive. Dissent was so severe and dangerous that Yasser seldom made public appearances.

We were forced to locate two Arabs to serve as look-alike doubles for him. We husbanded two of them because there would be many assassination attempts. If Yasser did get himself killed we would be ready to move one of the doubles into his place on stage so that the charade could continue as if nothing had happened.

Yasser loved the theater and couldn't resist being the showman. He even put on airs when he was just with his Western supporters. He had already received enough money to assure a comfortable retirement but he was not content. He demanded another five million dollars. He had the Western coalition over a barrel so they agreed. They arranged for the money to be delivered to him when he made his next public appearance in Jerusalem.

The incredible happened! The money was delivered to Yasser's suite in the hotel while he was away visiting his village. The suite was occupied by his double at the time. Yasser never got the money and the Western coalition never saw it again.

Yasser died suddenly under quite mysterious circumstances a short time later. Of course I know all about his death but I can't justify going into that just for the sake of relating an interesting story. Suffice it to say that it was inevitable-- he had outlived his usefulness and was a liability to everybody.

That lost payoff explains why I was in Jerusalem a year later. The last guy, who had my job as CIA Chief, had been unable to trace the money so Langley wanted me to take one last crack at it. They set me up for failure by asking me to track down money that had been missing for a year. I was equally pessimistic about finding the escaped Yasser double.

I figured anybody who was ugly enough to be able to pass as Yasser's double deserved some compensation in life. Besides, the double had earned the money for repeatedly exposing himself to assassination when acting as Yasser's double in public.

I was ready to give up the search when a lead came in that I felt obliged to follow. Somebody told one of our informants that he heard that some of the Palestinian *mullahs* (religious leaders) went for an extended visit to Karachi in Pakistan. One of the visitors came back and told our informant that an ugly looking man, living there, spoke Arabic fluently.

I sent out one of my local agents to investigate this Pakistani group and report back to me after a week. He said he went to daily payers and hung around the cafes but never saw anyone resembling Yasser. The day before he was scheduled to depart he enquired directly whether anyone had seen a man resembling his photo of Yasser.

Meanwhile, I was waiting comfortably in a nice East Jerusalem hotel. During the day I walked around the neighborhood and stopped for coffee several times. The food at the hotel was good but a nearby restaurant had food that was even better-- "As good as Mama used to make!"

I spent the evenings in the cabarets watching the singers and dancers. You can't say I was goofing off-- not doing my job. I was just supervising the activities of my agent from a distance. Even with my superior skills we were unable to pick up a promising direction to follow.

I had lots of time to think about this thankless mission that I was sent on. The money was lost before I came on the scene. I had been stationed in Paris at that time with no responsibility for what happened out there in Palestine. No, it was another CIA chief or State Department courier who had the reprimand in his folder--not me. What did I care if somebody else's balls were in a vise? I was more sympathetic toward the ugly Palestinian double, who was trying to find some contentment in life. Why should I pursue him?

I recalled my agent from Pakistan, and I left for Istanbul after debriefing him. I reported failure to my superior in Langley and silently wished my rich Palestinian a happy life. The money was never recovered as far as I know. I trust the five million was put to better use by the Palestinians than it would have with been by the US government.

THE WEST BANK

ONLY three times in my five-year tenure did I have to serve as tour guide for State Department couriers. I didn't mind; I loved to get out and travel, and share the simpler life that I knew as a child before I became important.

I have a desk job that rarely provides me with the opportunity to leave the office and get into the field. Most important messengers are State Department officials and protocol requires that they deliver their messages personally and openly; they don't need me sneaking around. Only rarely does a senior CIA officer accompany a courier throughout his mission.

My big nightmare would be to have to escort a White Anglo-Saxon Protestant into Arab territory. It would be even worse if he were a Jew or a born-again Christian with values to which I was opposed.

Three times I accompanied State Department couriers into enemy land. In their obituaries or vitae they were referred to as "Emissaries of the State Department."

These were dangerous times. The destruction of Palestinian homesteads and the replacement with Israeli settlements was at an all-time high; peace talks had been suspended repeatedly. Washington proposed a new round of peace talks and appointed another useless committee to pretend to search for an equitable arrangement.

This time the Americans didn't send an American Jew; instead, the chief fact-finder was a West Texas bible-thumper. Common sense would dictate the selection of a religiously neutral emissary but Israel and its supporters were powerful enough to prevent fairness from entering into diplomacy, You can be sure that Senator Mayo's campaign fund was sweetened by American Jewish money.

The State Department requested that the CIA increase the security arrangements during the Committee's visit. We couldn't just go out and add some off-duty Palestinian policemen to put on patrol. Increasing security in this case meant that regional security directors should deploy available personnel and accompany them to the hot spot.

I arrived in Jerusalem well before the arrival of the committee. The Senior Senator from Texas received me the next day at his hotel suite. To my surprise I liked him from the start. He was mild mannered-- not like the blustering West Texans often are. In fact he showed a gentleness seldom seen in Americans. I felt very sorry for the Senator when our abductors frightened him so much that he peed his pants.

Two men speaking Arabic were able to enter his suite with a passkey. They trained their guns on us before I could do anything. I just stood there waiting-- there was nothing else I could do. If there would be a place for heroics it would come later and at a time of my choosing.

The guys treated me roughly. When I joined the CIA I had contracted to give my life for America so I had already faced that prospect. I knew better than to plead for my life. I asked them to follow the international codes of decent treatment for their prisoners. I asked them not to shame us by behaving like savages—"All of us are children of Abraham!"

I confess that if I had been in their shoes I probably would have just shot us American spy bastards and not wasted much time about doing it. My thoughts gave me pause. Had I become such an animal that our enemies appeared heroic and decent? Which ones were the "bad guys?"

There was a legitimate reason for all this violence-- the Palestinians didn't trust Israeli intentions. Israel had signed an agreement to withdraw military protection from one of their new settlements and to return the Israeli residents to their old homes in the area. The Palestinians didn't trust the Israelis to be true to their word so they took us as hostages.

Once the abduction was completed the Palestinians proposed substituting a 10-million dollar guarantee for the hostages. The federal government seems to always be able to come up with money for foreign ops so they sent it by special courier from Washington. They imprisoned us in their camp for a couple of days until the money was received.

One of my more astute agents was able to follow the trail to the camp where we were being held hostage. He reported back to Langley and they authorized a Special Forces attack to liberate us. Our kidnapper and his relatives were all wiped out in a sudden attack before they had time to kill us hostages. The Senator and I were glad to be rescued but appalled at the price paid by our Arab "host." The 10 million was never recovered.

America called upon Israel to fulfill their part of the bargain to clear the settlements, but they reneged. They complained that the brokered talks had been biased and that the return of the land demanded by the Palestinians never really belonged to Arabs, anyway.

They walked away from the deal and left the Palestinians with the 10 million bucks to buy more weapons and to compensate the families of suicide bombers. I went back to my Istanbul office and tried to forget the dirty world I lived in. Once again, I thought-- "You're in the wrong business!"

When I read the first-hand account of Senator Mayo's detention by the Palestinians I was disappointed in all mankind. In an exclusive interview he left his hospital bed to tell the world about his suffering in the hands of these Godless animals. He told his constituents what they wanted to hear-- he lied. But I guess he was used to lying in his business, I know I was. After all he was a veteran politician just like I was a veteran spy and you learn to live with your own unforgivable actions.

But in all fairness we must acknowledge that we could never know what really was in the senator's heart. His few observations about his incarceration had been run through the spin masters and came out rather unrecognizable. I still liked the guy, but not the lies attributed to him.

EGYPT'S RENAISSANCE

EGYPTIANS overthrew the monarchy to institute a republic. The days were over for the notorious King Farouk and his extravagant 29 Cadillacs. The extremely popular Gamal Abdel Nasser was elected Egypt's president. His people met his nationalization of the Suez Canal with great acclaim. What looked like progress and empowerment to the Egyptians was viewed differently by the British and French owners of the Canal. They regarded these changes as the theft of their property and the beginning of a period of national confusion.

Reaction was almost immediate-- Israel invaded the Egyptian Sinai Peninsula and was backed by the British and French military. America stood by gleefully but was afraid to see the Europeans strengthen their control over the Middle East. The situation could be assessed more clearly in retrospect after things quieted down. It was apparent that Egypt was making important social and economic advances with Soviet help.

That was how things stood when I got a call from Abdullah, my buddy in the International Istanbul Police Force. What he told me on the phone piqued my interest-- I left the Embassy immediately. When I arrived at his office I found him staring at a golden breastplate of Pharaonic design-- it was breathtaking.

Abdullah explained that the breastplate had been discovered quite by accident and they had only started looking into its origins. He invited me to go with him to the Istanbul Museum of Antiquities to learn about it what we could.

The Director was astonished-- he was speechless for a minute or two. He mumbled a few words as he went over to a cabinet and took out a museum catalogue. He flipped through it until he reached the photo that revealed the same breastplate gleaming at us from the page. He recovered just enough to squeak out, "See?" The catalogue pictured and described the Tutankhamun treasures from the tomb in Upper Egypt.

The Director explained that the curator in Cairo divided the treasure into two parts when it was restored and ready for display. Only half the treasure would be on exhibit at any one time. This would keep the whole trove from being lost *en masse*. The piece before us was from the second portion of that treasure.

We turned to Abdullah for an explanation of how it came to be here in Istanbul. He started by telling us that he knew almost nothing about it. It was discovered quite unexpectedly when an Istanbuli shipping warehouse was being inventoried. The shipping company had been sued in another matter and the court had ordered an assessment of the contents of their rented warehouse.

This breastplate was the only object of a Pharaonic design that appeared during the warehouse assessment. The owner of the warehouse said that the package appeared to have originated in Alexandria, Egypt. A certain Istanbuli art collector was awaiting its delivery. Abdullah's eyes sparkled as he envisioned newspaper articles praising him for catching the thief of this fabled Egyptian national treasure.

Abdullah and I went to question the consignee but got nothing but denials. When Abdullah did accuse him of receiving stolen goods he was met with, "Some friend must have sent it as a surprise gift for me." We left with nothing and could only hope that the sender of the contraband might give evidence incriminating the consignee.

Abdullah turned to me with excitement over our new interest in life, "How would you like to take a little trip to Alexandria with me?" I said, sadly; "I don't think I could justify it. My country doesn't have any concern in this matter." He smiled sly and said, "I'll just put in my report that the consignee thought that a similar article may have been sent to NYC." I smiled back and said jokingly, "In that case I will be obliged to go to Egypt to follow up, won't I? Why don't we travel together?"

I had trouble getting to sleep that night. Abdullah and I had not worked a case together in more than a year. I thought to myself, "We really should spend more time together." As I lay awake, half dreaming, I recalled the romantic old days when violence and horror were confined to comic books; now they were all too real. My wandering imagination magically transformed Abdullah and me into the "Champions of Justice"-- **Istanbul's Secret Warriors**.

We flew to Alexandria the next day. I love the second largest city of Egypt. It has a major harbor and the people are very unlike those in Cairo. Of course, Alexandria was named after Alexander the Great, who stopped over there on his travels. The city was a Greek colony even before it became a Roman satrapy.

The superficial aspects of being Greek have disappeared-- the people are Arabicized, but the Greek blood lies not too far beneath the surface. Many residents still think of themselves as being Greek even though they were born in Egypt. The cultural mix makes for an interesting milieu.

Alexandrian food and entertainment are the best in the world so we headed straight away for a restaurant, and later, a cabaret. We retired early because we expected to be busy the following day; we were wrong. The next morning we finished our work in less than an hour.

We walked to the harbor and located the address of the consigner of the breastplate. All we found was an empty lot at the address we were seeking. There was little reason to question the simple stand owner next door who sold talafel (fried bean cakes). It was obvious that the consignor's address had been pulled out of a hat.

The next day we took a trip to Cairo to talk with the Curator of the Cairo Museum. Cairo is a nice city to visit but the traffic is unbearable. Walking is dangerous and even going a couple of miles by taxi takes forever.

The national police welcomed us properly. Eventually we got down to business and it started off with a bang. Abdullah opened the container and exposed the breastplate-- we watched the Curator's face. Sure enough, his eyes widened, his breathing stopped and he turned white. He was answering some of our questions without speaking a word!

The curator told us that our piece was supposed to be locked up in the hypobaric room with its companion pieces. He explained that each of the two treasure lots was kept in separate rooms with moisture and barometric pressure carefully controlled. Both rooms were securely guarded and he was the only person allowed to enter unaccompanied.

He swore that it was impossible for someone to have removed the breastplate without his knowledge. He believed our piece was a copy until he finished examining it. Then he shook his head in chagrin and turned to us and said, "It's authentic. It's the very piece I placed in the vault room myself. I recognize some small scratches on the clasp." It didn't occur to any of us at the time to check to see if any additional artifacts were missing from either of the two treasure vaults. We just assumed that they were well protected by the electronic security devices.

We were all in a quandary-- what should we do next? There was only one direction still open to us-- to check security precautions. The Curator called in the head of security service and ordered him to give his full cooperation to us in trying to solve the mystery of this theft.

We spent two days talking to personnel and studying their folders. This was no easy job because just about everybody with a menial government job is poor. So we couldn't narrow the list of suspects by selecting the poor ones, those who most needed to sell out their employer.

We decided to go back to Istanbul and see if we could open a lead on that end because we were getting nowhere in Egypt. The night before we left Cairo we had dinner together and then sat around drinking brandy. About all we ever talked about was work because we didn't have much other life. Sitting and talking was often helpful. We looked idle but we were not.

Some small thing in the affair poked its head out, begging to be noticed. Then it struck me. There was a similarity in names between one of the employees and the proprietor of the Alexandrian falafel stand, next to the phony consigner's address.

We cancelled our flight reservations, renewed our stay at the hotel, and hustled back to the museum. I found the employee's name as I leafed through the personnel folders of the museum. His name was Ibrahim Khalil.

As you already know, the first label is the individual's name and the second is the father's name. (Family names are rarely used, like in the west). We were disappointed that the name of father and son were such common ones. Furthermore the two father-son names customarily appear together as a pair so that the father with the name Khalil often would name his son Ibrahim. The father with the name Ibrahim would name his son Khalil. We realized that a high percentage of the population were Khalil Ibrahim and Ibrahim Khalil.

What was even worse was that I couldn't remember the name of the falafel vender-- was it Khalil Ibrahim or was it Ibrahim Khalil? That meant we had to shift our investigation back to Alexandria; at that point we had no good reason to stay in Cairo. The next day found us back in the same hotel in Alexandria. Guess where we ate that night? Right! We ate falafel at Khalil Ibrahim's sidewalk stand.

I took a bold, direct approach, "We met your son, Ibrahim Khalil, at the Cairo Museum. He asked us to give you his love." The response was all we could have hoped for. Khalil burst into a broad grin and wanted to know all about our visit to Cairo, "Where did you meet Ibrahim? Is he alright? Does he like his job any better?" We bluffed our way though. Then I got bold again and revealed that we were tracking down a package that bore the neighboring address.

He thought a little-- probably he was stalling for time. He admitted that Ibrahim had visited him the previous weekend and gave him a package to post. Ibrahim addressed the package and used the neighbor for a return address. Khalil swore he had no knowledge of what was in the package. That was all the information he gave us.

We had to rush back to Cairo to confront Ibrahim before he escaped. This time we had a super lead. We wasted no time interrogating him. He knew he was caught and so he told us what he could. A colleague from Alexandria gave Ibrahim the package to mail while he was visiting his father. He didn't have any idea what was in it, but he was curious that the sender had gone through all this trouble to remain unknown.

The Director called the police and Ibrahim was placed in custody. We might need to question him again to get any information that he was holding back. We grabbed his confederate before he left his station at the museum. The confederate spoke Arabic with a perfect Egyptian accent despite bearing the Greek name Stavros.

We conducted the interview because we knew more than the Egyptian police about what was going on. But from this point on we included the local and national police in everything we did. We saw that this affair was snowballing and felt more secure with the police at our back.

Stavros admitted taking the breastplate from the lot of items after an exhibit when he was assisting the Director restock them. He told us that he did it out of fear more than for the money. "The cheap bastards only gave me a thousand dollars to steal something worth millions. I wouldn't have done it if 'they' hadn't threatened to kill my son."

Stavros wouldn't tell us who "they" were. He said they would kill him and his son if he gave them up to the police. We left the room and let the police question him.

An hour later we returned to the interrogation room. Stavros looked battered and subdued but he told the police what we all needed to know.

Stavros said that the ones behind the robbery were acquaintances from Alexandria, who lived near the falafel stand. He gave us half a dozen names but they meant nothing to us at that time. He described the malcontents. They were Greeks who resented the arbitrary rule of the monarchy and didn't trust any other Egyptians to treat the Greeks fairly.

He said, "They want to go back to the old ways of government. I didn't know what he meant so I asked him to clarify. Then he told us the most unbelievable thing he could possibly come up with, "They want to restore the rule of the Ptolemys." I was shocked! What? Turn the clock back 2,000 years to the time of the pharaohs?" Those were the old days of Greco-Roman hegemony in the Mediterranean, the days of Julius Cesar, and of Mark Antony and Cleopatra.

At this point Stavros was sent back to his cell to lick his wounds. The Cairo police deferred to the National Security Services to follow up on the names that Stavros had mentioned as conspirators. Of course the National Police had their Alexandrian office check out those suspected of complicity and had a report for us by the following morning.

The conspirators were members of a radical Greek political party that the National Police had infiltrated and had been watching for the past few years. They had become more active lately. The police thought that some new leadership in the party had energized the members. The resurgence of Greco-Roman imperialism would have to wait a few more centuries, at least.

Almost a hundred years earlier the monarchy reopened the ancient Pharaonic salt mines in the Nubian Desert to provide suitable punishment for treasonous subjects. They were still operating and ready to receive Ibrahim and his co-conspirator in Cairo as well as those from Alexandria.

IRAQ

I SAT ON the wooden grating on the floor of the shower, embracing and cuddling myself. I was alone like I am most of the time-- alone to recall the horrors of the day.

I could still hear the splat, like a bundle of wet laundry striking against the floor. I began scrubbing my body again to get rid of any remaining debris. I imagined that I was still stained with the crimson blood of the man, who died in my arms. I scrubbed away at the grey brain tissue that I imagined had penetrated the pores of my skin. Authors of fiction would try to disguise the horror of my images by using a gimmicky word like "Flashback."

Woops! Sorry, I forget that I'm one of the tough guys. I'm a survivor. The State Department suits consist of diplomats, politicians, and minor desk-jockeys. When they have to grapple with the real world they need field agents like those of us who are burnished by the friction with the real world.

* * * * *

Iraq was going to hell-- nothing could stop it. We Westerners had limited power to deflect the anger of the people and redirect their aspirations along the lines that would benefit us.

Baghdad was in political turmoil and I was in the midst of it. The protests and demonstrations of 1942 were long over. The repressive government hanged the leaders of the coup and left their corpses at the city gates to draw flies. Nothing had been achieved by the attempted coup except a small note in history:

"In 1942 the Prime Minister El-Gailani declared war on Britain. The skirmish near Baghdad at Lake Habaniya finished that short war and re-established the monarchy."

By coincidence I was being sent on a mission that would take me to the historic battlefield at Habaniya. I was sent there by the American government as part of the security team protecting the national representatives to a meeting of a Baghdad Pact committee dealing with the Middle East. The committee was being entertained at King Faisal's resort at Lake Habaniya, not far from Baghdad.

When we arrived I stepped out of the military carrier and made a visual security scan. Then I assisted our load of guests to climb out of the vehicle. The crack of a sniper's rifle startled us. The man standing next to me slumped against me and we sank to the ground together. It was as though someone had just turned a hot shower on me. The victim's blood gushed out of the place where his face used to be, but only for the few seconds he remained alive.

I retrieved my sidearm and looked for the enemy. I spotted him perched on the rim of the roof of a nearby building. As I approached the assassin's position I was pushed aside by the guards. Then what I knew would happen did happen. The soldiers killed the assassin in a hail of rifle bullets.

They had destroyed the most important evidence at the scene. They took out the one link that could have led us directly and quickly to those behind the killing. In my line of work you learn to be suspicious of everyone and everything. At the time I wondered if the destruction of that link might not have been the main purpose of the barrage.

I looked over the other arriving passengers as I went to clean myself and borrow some fresh clothes. A man rode up in another vehicle; he had to be important because his several bodyguards surrounded him to form a screen. He looked familiar. Yes, I recognized him from my files back in Istanbul-- he was the Iraqi Prime Minister, Nuri Said.

I looked at him again and did a quick retake. He looked like the man from my van who was just shot. Of course! I knew immediately what had happened. Nuri Said was the target of the assassination but the sniper shot the prime minister's stand-in instead.

After showering I dressed and reported to the head of security. I offered my assistance and he thanked me. He asked me to compile lists of every one of the visitors, who had arrived before or at the time of the shooting. The Baghdad Pact committee held a brief meeting and then adjourned for the day, but held themselves available for questioning and debriefing.

In the course of the subsequent hour every one memorized what to say to outsiders, "It was all simply a misunderstanding. Two feuding soldiers got into a disagreement and started a shoot-out in which they killed one another."

The Police and Secret Service knew very well that the intent had been to kill the prime minister and make way for a new government. They did not hesitate to lie to their citizens and the whole world. Funny isn't it that officials think that witnesses and suspects must tell them the truth, but that the government is free to lie on a much grander scale. They weren't kidding me. I saw the picture of the intended target that the investigators removed from the pocket of the shooter. Of course, it was a newspaper picture of Nuri Said.

The secret services contradicted the first, benign account of the shooting. They had to operate with a more truthful scenario, "Somebody tried to assassinate Nuri Said and the parties responsible would be routed out of society."

The police and secret service agents joined in a dragnet of Baghdad. They brought in all known political dissidents for questioning. I couldn't imagine what they expected to accomplish from such a bull-in-the-china shop approach. The only intelligent thing they did do was to offer a large reward for information leading to the capture of the culprits behind the shooting.

I cleared my plan with the secret services. I was going to search for a local lead while they were wasting their time in Baghdad. Perhaps I was influenced by the venue-- Habaniya was a paradise compared to bustling, Baghdad. I got as far away from the official confusion as possible and settled in for a few days. You need a little time for your face to become a little familiar before people will talk to you.

All the citizens were talking about the shooting. The killer was praised in low voices-- nobody seemed to like Nuri or the government. None of this was news but I sat around hoping somebody would slip something useful into the conversation.

I noticed something strange that week. An unusual number of people visited two adjacent houses in a district near my hotel. I saw people coming and going every time I went for a walk there. I asked the owner of a neighboring café about it. He said casually, "Their son just died recently."

I thought to myself, "Visits to offer condolences should finish after the third day but in this case it seemed like they are increasing in frequency." I asked around a little, but I was careful not to overload any one source for answers. I was able to string little bits of things together until I had a fairly good picture of what went on.

The dead man couldn't give us a confession so we could close the case. We would have to depend upon his family to confirm what happened. Fortunately, none of the police had made the family wary so I was able to begin a friendship with a young man from the family in question.

We agreed on politics. We both hated the British colonial mastery that used Nuri to govern Iraq. I was right there with the rest of the citizens praising the martyr who tried to bring Nuri down. "The poor boy was a hero and we should all say prayers for him!"

We both saw politics in a similar manner despite being on opposite sides of the law. I believed that the risk of revealing myself would be worth it to settle this case.

My local friend and I went to my hotel and we enjoyed a good meal together. Then I got him to promise in advance to listen to what I had to say for five minutes without interrupting. He agreed. I did a reconstruction:

"It was your relative, probably a brother, who attempted to assassinate Nuri Said. I don't know his name or even how he was employed. Your family and all of Iraq will remember him for what he tried to do for his people. He died a hero and a martyr. His will be the glory on the Judgement Day!

The clothes he was wearing at the time of his death were borrowed and untraceable. The rifle was standard army issue and nondescript. Nobody in your town would ever betray him. Anyone who dared to give him away would be in danger of losing his own life.

I know these things but I have no reason to report my suspicions to anyone because I have no real proof. If I planned to betray your brother I wouldn't be placing myself at your mercy by telling you these things. We have become friends and I know you to be a fair and intelligent man, so I trust you."

He extended his hand and said, "We are at your mercy." I shook it and told him, "I would like to pay a sympathy call to your family; your brother deserves that. Instead, I will leave the city today because I don't want to provide any links to your family that the Secret Service might follow."

As I boarded the plane to return to Istanbul the following day, I reflected upon the irony of fate. Everything is relative; nothing is absolute. What is evil one day is good the next. What is treasonous one day is patriotic the next.

NEUTRON BOMB

I WAS startled by the news when I arrived at my office in the morning. Everybody but me knew that the Russians had dropped a nuclear bomb on Turkey! I couldn't believe it, but there was the story, right on the front page-- "Russia Drops Nuclear Bomb on Turkey! Parliament to Meet in Emergency Session. Prime Minister to Ask Approval for Retaliation on Russia."

This was the first day of the strange drama that was unfolding. Everybody in Turkey switched to an emergency wartime footing, especially in all the embassies. The future had suddenly become wholly unpredictable. I ordered all my people stationed in and around Istanbul to retreat to the Embassy. As they say, "The shit hit the fan!" It was a time to close ranks.

Anytime I have to confront a serious crisis I think of my police lieutenant friend, Abdullah. We enjoy each other's company and like working together. Since America was not involved directly in this present incident I would have no official reason to assist in the investigation.

I wasn't even sure Abdullah still had any responsibility. Martial law may have suspended his police authority. If the Turkish parliament declared war then all matters of that sort would revert to the military. But, until that time Abdullah would be under pressure to provide information to his government.

I phoned Abdullah and offered my sympathy and my assistance. I asked, "Do you need my help?" He exploded on the phone, "Hell, yes!" I told him, "I'll drop everything and be right there."

I made a mad dash down the *Corniche* avenue along the Bosphorus Sea. Thirty minutes later we were exchanging embraces and sympathetic looks. My own office was in an upheaval so I brought along an assistant to provide liaison with the rest of my gang. I was going to refer to them as my "employees," but somehow that doesn't describe them quite as well as my "gang."

* * * * *

The Early Warning System at the Samsun airbase sounded the alarm when an unidentified bomber drifted into Turkish air space. The plane was flying from west to east while hugging the boundary between Russian air space and the Turkish. The plane seemed to have drifted a little into Turkish space by accident.

Two Turkish fighters were scrambled but they only pursued the unidentified bomber a few miles. Both pilots thought the invader was a Russian bomber, but maybe they saw what they were expecting to see. The bomber made a sharp turn to the south out over the southern coastline of the Black Sea. Within a few minutes a bomb of considerable force exploded. The nuclear cloud that formed at the drop site was recognized from the airbase so the two fighters were recalled.

The base went on full alert. Everybody either went to his post to man the ground defences or sought protective shelter. This was no drill!

Military reports indicated that the bomb drop was on a small deserted island in the Black Sea near the coastal city of Samsun. Reports of damage or casualties were unknown because the island was relatively unpopulated. Residents on the shore near the island affirmed that the main casualties would be among the wild goats. The newspapers speculated that the Russians spared lives to indicate that the bombing was meant more as a warning than as a provocation to all-out war.

The order went out to close all the Turkish embassies in Russian territories and in the Soviet satellites. Everybody was trying to get his house in order. The next day Russia released a denial that they had committed such a perfidy, especially since, "Turkey is such a good friend and neighbor-- " the usual bullshit diplomatic phrases.

It took another whole day before Russia had the courage to disseminate a lie to cover their treachery. They announced that the Big Satan, America dropped the bomb so that Russia would be blamed.

It seemed like everybody in Istanbul, who could justify it, wanted to fly to the Samsun scene. Some of the members of parliament tried to crowd us out of our plane seats to Samsun. We refused to give up our seats because trained investigators were needed on site, not sightseers.

The existing situation was very serious and should have been recognized as such by all Turks. The army provided us with quarters and access to the officers' mess. We were comfortable enough to be able to do our job properly, and that's what came first at such a critical time.

We knew we wouldn't get much reliable information. There were few residents near the bombsite available to report first-hand observations. We asked a few questions and found out that the Samsun newspaper was even more reliable than our informants-- the newspaper was less subject to hysterical exaggeration.

Turkish reconnaissance planes that flew over the bombsite established that it was radioactive so we were in no hurry to approach it. Still we had to learn what we could about the bombsite. High over-flights indicated that the nuclear activity would not be fatal if we didn't fly too low and we limited our time directly over the site to just a couple of minutes.

We equipped ourselves with radioactivity counters and telescopic scopes and cameras. Then we took off in a helicopter from the Samsun airbase. We were careful to maintain altitude above 20,000 feet at the site. We felt we would be safe from serious radiation effects if we limited our exposure to making only one pass. Ten minutes after takeoff we were ready to stare down into the jaws of death. We did our job and made the pass, snapping pictures automatically.

Upon return to the Samsun base we developed the pictures. We already saw on the site the evidence we needed, but now we had it on photographic plates as well. Near the blast site was the cargo door of the invading bomber. It lay right-side-up and the Soviet emblem was clearly visible.

I asked Abdullah if something special was going on between Turkey and Russia. He didn't know of anything. He agreed that the use of a radioactive bomb by Russia could be no accident. We realized that there was something important we didn't know about. Perhaps Russia sent an emphatic message earlier that the Turks had ignored?

We could expect to make little progress while the diplomats were pondering that charade. Once again we had a tangled skein and had no idea where to find the end of the yarn to begin unravelling it.

The Turkish ordinance people brought in nuclear physicists. From the crater and the pattern of radiation they were sure that the bomb was a neutron type. That kind of bomb had a very intense, but confined, radiation pattern. Such bombs were rather passé, replaced by other more destructive ones. The Turkish government could assure the populace that there was little fear of spreading radiation-- it would have already done the small amount of damage that it would do.

This information about the nature of the bomb puzzled me. The bombing looked more and more like only a warning. What was so important that Russia wanted to warn the Turkish army and the nation about? What called for such a bizarre attack? By using a radioactive bomb they had disturbed world peace in a way that was universally unacceptable; it would upset everybody.

America may have been able to get away with nuking Japan twice, but that was a long time ago. Since then, there has been a sort of gentlemen's agreement not to be the one who throws the first stone. Now Russia's action had provoked the whole world.

Military actions usually make some kind of sense but not this time. Why did the Russians employ such a complicated offensive action? Why didn't they just bomb the Ministry of Defence or the Prime Minister's office? Also, there were plenty of ships in the Bosphorus Sea that they could have bombarded.

We couldn't investigate the scene any closer up because it would remain radioactive for years. We had no access to the offenders and their destructive tools because they probably were all back in Russia. We wouldn't be able to come up with any physical evidence sitting on our duffs there in Turkey. We could alert our spies in Russia and have them seek an answer but that would take time.

We were going to have to put the case in the "Inactive file" and go home. We would leave it to the newspapers and the diplomats to point the accusatory fingers. On the way back to Istanbul I wondered, "Why would a cargo door fall off their bomber? Could it be a coincidence that it fell off right at the place the plane dropped its bomb?"

The Western allies kept poking their fingers in Russia's face but they continued to deny having anything to do with the bombing. For months the Turkish press wrote about nothing except Russian atrocities. The Turks in the street were ready to go to war to save their country. The Russian press editorials were all the same. They accused America and Turkey of being in the plot to discredit the Russians. The Russians in the street were ready to go to war with everybody to save their good name.

* * * * *

Do you know how to play chess? If your answer is, "Yes," then I would say that the CIA needs your services. When you make a move in a game of chess it is designed to weaken your opponent's game, right? When the other opponent takes his turn, his move will be directed at spoiling your game. Adversary spy agencies play a similar kind of game.

"Can you image chess opponents being able to find that a single move would advance both of their games? But that is exactly what happened in our Cold War chess game, when somebody dropped that neutron bomb in an open field on the deserted island in the Black Sea."

For the next six months both countries were on a wartime footing. Military recruitment was up and morale in both armies was higher than it had been in a long time. The politicians were able to increase taxes and order more modern and expensive weapons. Military officers were promoted in rank. Both governments printed more money and pseudo prosperity forged ahead. The approval levels of the leaders in both countries rose to new highs. Even the donations to Amnesty International and Red Cross rose more than 50 percent.

* * * * *

Suddenly the house of cards came tumbling down. One of my agents in Turkey asked to meet me in Istanbul because he had some very important information about the Samsun bombing. He was right about it being important-- it was world-shaking!

My agent knew how we in the CIA play games with the truth, and he knew how little we value it. He asked me, "Are you sure you want to open up the Samsun neutron bombing case?" I moaned and braced myself; then I encouraged him to continue.

He said he was visiting with another of our agents in a bar. The agent had quite a lot to drink and was feeling his oats. He started bragging that he was the only person in all of Turkey, who really knew what happened at Samsun. "To this day even the Turkish Prime Minister doesn't know!"

I thought that what I was listening to was so much barroom bullshit. Then he started bringing together the pieces of his story and I was dumbfounded. I asked him, "This agent is called Gary, right?" It looked like my agent Gary was withholding information from me and may even have been involved in a secret conspiracy that almost caused a war. No way could I let this go by. I summoned him to Istanbul without delay.

I didn't even trust the security of my own office for conducting the interview with Gary. When he entered my office I refused to shake hands with the deceitful bastard. I told him straight out, "You're in deep shit! You need to tell me everything and don't lie or hold back anything if you want my help." We went out in the garden and this is what he told me:

"Two months ago you assigned me to work undercover as an aircraft mechanic at the Incirlik Air Base watching for protest groups and sabotage. One day I was ordered to report to the Major's office where I met a middle-age gent in civies. I saluted him anyway, as I did the major. They both acknowledged my salute. They not only ordered me "at ease" but also invited me to sit down with them.

I learned that the "suit" was a member of our government in Washington. I was cautioned not to inquire about the higher-ups, who issued my new orders. I was to work under the suit's orders only, and the major would supply whatever would be required to accomplish my assignment.

I would be in charge of one other person, a pilot, who would be supplied by the major at the right time. I was responsible for the upcoming mission and should know that I was backed at the highest possible level. I was too intimidated to ask who was backing me, so I just listened.

I would continue to work as a mechanic to provide my cover but I would no longer be responsible to the CIA. I was explicitly told that neither you nor your agents were to know that I was working for the White House.

At two different times I was given packets of instructions. The first concerned a captured Russian bomber, which was stored on the Incirlik base in a secure hanger. I was to restore it to flying condition. The plane needed to be only airworthy for 100 hours flying time. A rear cargo door was to be removed and stored separately in the hold for use in the second part of my mission.

When the plane was ready I received the second and final instructions. I was to telephone a number and arrange for the man who answered to meet me at Incirlik base. He was the pilot, who would conduct a final flight check.

I phoned him and he joined me so we could do the flight check together. He approved the condition of the plane and we were ready to fly to our destination early the following morning.

I had all the information needed about flying the mission and the detached cargo door was stored inside so that it could be jettisoned. I served as navigator.

We flew low along the border with Iran and broke out over the Black Sea near the Turkish airbase at Samsun. We located the target island and jettisoned our detached cargo door and a bomb simultaneously.

The bomb was so powerful that it drove us up several thousand feet higher in altitude and then bounced us around like an autumn leaf. We took the plane out into open water and ditched it, as instructed. A patrol boat had been pre-positioned and it picked us up and brought us to a village where we found a jeep waiting to get us back to Incirlik. We were severely cautioned to never talk with any of the persons we encountered on our mission.

I went back to my CIA cover at the Incirlik base and the pilot went about his business. We never acknowledge knowing each other whenever we met accidentally. Nobody except my major and the White House knew the nature of our mission.

We realized from the start that the operation would be the biggest hoax ever perpetrated. We also realized that our lives could be endangered if we talked, since the whole world was being suckered.

He was apologetic. Boss, I want to tell you how sorry I am about having to conceal my mission from you, even though you were my superior."

The next day I was on a flight to Washington to demand an explanation why the suits were controlling my agents without my knowledge. I had my signed resignation in my pocket.

Those smart bastards at State pre-empted me. As soon as I showed up the Secretary of State greeted me with, "Congratulations on a job well done!" He explained that the mission had to be protected with the highest security level of clearance. It just wouldn't do for it to get out that the head of our government had approved such a circus act and made fools of the whole world!

I'm a sucker for a bureaucrat's smile and a pat on the back. Before I could get my resignation out of my pocket I was being congratulated for my increase in civil service grade. What the hell! I went into the executive dining room and had lunch with the Secretary of State before going back to my dumb old job.

KARBALA

I WAS off guard after a pleasant meal in a downtown hotel in Baghdad. I was relaxed and at peace with the world; unfortunately, the world was not at peace with me. As I stood outside the door of my room I heard the scraping sounds of drawers being pulled open and slid shut. It wouldn't be the first time my rooms were searched.

The real concern was that I was no longer controlling my environment-- in my business that can be fatal. I was on a secret mission-- I'm always on a secret mission except when I'm back home in my Istanbul headquarters. Even there I have to remain in control most of the time.

Maybe it was a simple theft and I wouldn't want to give up my cover for such a small matter. I decided not to burst into the room with gun held at ready. When you're a spy you learn to reverse matters to your advantage. I knocked gently on the door and announced, "Room service."

The door opened a crack. I was ready to grasp my automatic and pull the trigger until all danger was dissipated. Then I saw the startled face of my friend Jonathan. I relaxed and smiled, "Why the hell didn't you tell me you needed my shaving cream! I nearly shot you."

Jonathan was an old friend and colleague from MI6, the British equivalent of CIA. We used to see each other every so often when we were out in the field. Lately, the instability of the Middle East resulted in our being called out for urgent service-- we kept bumping into each other everywhere.

I liked seeing him. I lived a lonely life and even having a spy for company is better than having no company at all. If we had met earlier in the hotel it would have made dinner just that much more enjoyable. I was about to offer him a scotch but I noticed the bottle was already open and a glass had been half-filled with the amber liquid. He said, "If I had known this was your room I would have poured out a drink for you, too."

Jonathan smiled and I forgave him his presumptuousness. Turning to me he said, "I mistook you for somebody I'm supposed to check on-- a Brit using an alias. I was studying your possessions to see if you were he. Unfortunately I didn't find anything worth stealing!"

He continued, "But I did find you, old chap, and that's better than having to deal with some other more disagreeable person. I have to go down to the city of Karbala tomorrow, can you come with me? I'd love the company and you know the city better than I do." I told him that I would enjoy a diversionary trip with him. He was very pleased.

The next morning Jonathan's driver arrived at the hotel in a light military vehicle. He brought along Jonathan's bodyguard *cum* assistant. We couldn't leave the loaded vehicle in the street because the cargo was very valuable. We all had a good breakfast and then loaded the truck. We were carrying the annual payoffs that Jonathan was taking to the seven sheiks of the Karbala region.

There was not much to see and even less to do on the ride down south. Jonathan asked me to brief him on Karbala and its historic importance in the Muslim religion.

First you need to clarify a few terms. *Khalif* (Caliph) is Arabic for follower or successor of Mohammed. The Khalif was the ruler of the whole religious and sectarian Muslim world-- sort of like a Pope. The first four Khalifs were uncontested and are undisputed to this day."

The forth Khalif, named Ali, lost the leadership to a powerful contender, who then started a new line of Khalifs that continues to have the support of the majority of Muslims right up to the present time. These followers are called *Sunna,* which means the "orthodox" ones in Arabic.

The splinter group, the supporters of Ali, still dispute the Sunni right of succession to political leadership. This disgruntled minority is called *Shi'i.* These *Shi'a* (plural) live mostly in southern Iraq and Iran. The Shi'a tend to obscure the basic elements of Islam by adding their own observances to the Muslim religious practices.

The city of Karbala contains the unbelievably magnificent shrine of Hussein, son of Ali. Hussein was the martyred leader, who should have succeeded his father. Instead, the Sunna martyred him and all his family and followers in Karbala.

The graves of Ali and his sons became holy shrines and the destination for Shi'i pilgrims. They have elaborated their Muslim beliefs and practices with mystical additions. They emphasize the importance of a pilgrimage to Karbala and the veneration of the tombs of the religious leaders. They hold annual processions to commemorate the torturing of Hussein by his enemies. Their myths extend to the belief that their last leader, from centuries ago, will mysteriously reappear some day.

The history of a schism is seldom a pretty one. The struggle of the Shi'a for the freedom to express their beliefs and practices is not just a religious matter. The schism has a disgraceful political history-- the bloody victory of the oppressive majority over the righteous few.

Like most Turkish families, my own has always followed the orthodox Sunni practices but I find these Shi'i rites and beliefs interesting. When we go to the shrines we will see pilgrims from all parts of the world, but mostly from Iran. The Shi'a have built the most beautiful mosque-like structures in the world to venerate their "saints."

We Sunna can appreciate the Shi'i shows of honor and devotion but we are more comfortable with our own basic, simple, orthodox worship of God.

We certainly could have chosen a better time to go to Karbala. Most of the million pilgrims had arrived in Karbala but the roads leading there still were jammed with the multitudes. Our trip was going to take most of the day.

Jonathan certainly could have concluded his business at a better time, but then we would have missed all the primitive pageantry. In four days the peak of activity would engulf people and city entirely. It would be the holiest day of the year-- called *Ashura*.

The political ferment of 1200 years ago was still alive throughout the world and threatening our well-being. The players for political power had changed but it was the same old game-- the martyrs against the oppressors. The Shi'a play the Holocaust and Genocide cards that were so successfully used in the West in the mid twentieth century.

We were jostled and deafened by the press of people. More than a million adherents were marching into a town, normally supporting 50,000

I remonstrated with my Karbala brothers,

"Do you live in the past to improve the present? Wouldn't it be better to dedicate your lives to improving the existence of your Shi'i brothers, or even of the Sunna? Does your tearing of flesh and rending of clothes benefit you or your brothers? Do your actions spread contentment and satisfaction to those brothers who seek a better life?"

They should learn how to look inward at the soul rather than outward for enemies-- turn misery into joy. Their religion evolved into a masochistic perversion. I was reminded of the old children's stories from the Orient about prisoners being tortured to death by the tickles of a feather. I hoped we would fare better.

This is not what I expect from my religion-- I want my religion to enhance my life. Oh well, to each his own. Each person's life is his to expend as he wishes.

Only God and His prophets have the right to tell us how to live it.

The truth seems to be that we can work together to help one another in this difficult life or we can be obstructive and quarrelsome and never know the blessings of God.

We parked the car at the governor's mansion where we would be accommodated. Jonathan and I carried the treasure to our quarters inside, while Jonathan's two men guarded the truck from the hundreds of fingers that poked and probed it. Finally we were unloaded and removed from the raging, roaring crowd. We sat on a shaded balcony and sipped tea and watched the world rush on below us.

Another guest at the governor's mansion offered us cigars. We were pleased to accept them. He was a pleasant looking person whose clothes and manner reflected gentility. He could have been the leader of a tribe or just a landowner. He said that he was simply a traveler and had never had the chance to see the Ashura in Karbala, before. He asked us what brought us there.

In the spy business you learn not to betray your status by being evasive. Hesitation gives you away-- you have to be ready to lie glibly. We told him that we were on our way to the city of Basra to buy dates for export and we stopped over a bit because of the heavy press of travelers.

My interlocutor had an unusual accent. He spoke formal Arabic correctly but his difficulty in understanding colloquial Arabic exposed him as a spy. This illustrated one of the weaknesses in the Israeli cadres who try to penetrate and subvert the Arab societies. They may have lived with the Arabs as neighbors and learned to imitate them, but their own petty gestures or habits are always there to betray their Jewish origin. Similarly, they may learn to speak the slang but fail to accompany it with appropriate little gestures. Our chatty companion was a troublemaker, an *agent provocateur*. How could I tell? As they say, "It takes one to know one."

Jonathan apologized for being unable to spend more time with me during the day. He complained,

"Since the Mossadegh revolution in Iran and the el-Gailani in Baghdad, I am nothing more than a paymaster to support British influence. We spend millions of British pounds each year trying to keep the Arabs dependent, yet happy.

We still honor some of the old ways based in patronage even though Iraq is technically an independent kingdom. Iraqis have their own governing system and sources of revenue but we have never completely discontinued the feudal custom of the lord offering his support."

He went on to explain,

"I will have to meet with the leaders (Sheikhs) of the seven local tribes to pledge our mutual loyalty. Each sheikh is allowed to raise just only one unresolved legal issue to be settled by my adjudication. I never studied Law but I am here acting as judge to prevent their quarrels from further disrupting the peace.

They only accept my interference in their affairs because of the gold I deliver to them at the conclusion of our meetings. I'll give each of them a large stipend after settling their jurisdictional complaints about one another They don't all understand the value of financial instruments written on paper so we pay them in British gold sovereigns."

Jonathan explained further,

"I will meet the sheikhs individually in the governor's office but no witnesses will be summoned, only my interpreter will be there to serve the court. I'm sorry that I can't invite you to attend. The whole thing is secret the meetings will never have taken place. These proud leaders must be able to deny ever meeting with foreigners and being told what to do.

The disputes are seldom important, but always interesting. I can trust you so I will tell you about the complaints in the evenings after the conferences."

I reassured Jonathan, "I brought along my favorite history book to give me something to do. How many times have your read Philip Hitti's, <u>History of the Arabs</u>?" He replied, "Twice-- it's the number one textbook back in Whitehall spy school."

Jonathan rambled on-

"Things out here are changing fast. We are in the middle of the 20th century; some of the people we have to deal with have Ph.D.'s in Political Science. The, 'You likee pretty beads?' era is gone forever. I behave like a gentleman and expect respect in return when on business in the Middle East. I never am lulled into thinking that my meetings are with real friends; each of us has his own agenda."

Jonathan explained his schedule:

"The first day I meet all the sheiks and hear any complaints and issues they may have. They are a contentious people and they always are bitching about something. The second day I review the evidence relating to the issues raised in the complaints. The third day I make the pronouncements that the sheikhs are bound to accept without appeal. On the fourth day I deliver the gold coins that resonate so pleasantly in the ears of those desert Arabs."

* * * * *

The next day the pilgrims in the street entertained me. "Entertained" is not the correct word for it-- "amazed" would be more accurate. Young men, and even the old, staggered along the streets and lanes of the city. They were testing to see how much suffering their bodies could tolerate. They would beat the mourning-drums and slap their backs with metal chains. Some of the pilgrims desired more intense punishment so they fastened pieces of razor-like metal onto the chains. They took pride in displaying the torn flesh and rivulets of blood on their shoulders and backs.

They knew they had reached the condition that would permit them to empathize with the martyrs of yesteryear when they could stand no more of the self-immolation. They are imbued with the desire to understand Hussein's suffering. Accompanying this is the need to be punished for the deeds committed in the old days by the Faithful. Some of their Muslim ancestors caused Hussein's suffering and others stood by and let it happen. Present-day descendents feel guilty even though it happened so long ago and their kinship is remote.

* * * * *

Jonathan came to supper that night, but he was worn out. He had been in conference with the sheikhs all day. I begged him to share with me what came up in his meetings; so he told me--

"The first case dealt with an old issue, but one that is hard to settle. If the solution were simple then the matter would not keep on resurfacing.

The sheikh claimed that those in the neighboring district were stealing water from his wells. Those from the other tribe helped themselves with the approval of their sheikh. He reassured his people that water belongs to no one but God and didn't discourage this stealing.

I recognized justification in both positions. At the same time I realized that there was a face-saving issue that should be addressed. My judgment affirmed that water was the gift of God for all mankind. All are entitled to take water but if it is from another person's well then he must do so with permission.

If another tribe dug out the well on land that is within their district then tribal members have first call on the waters. But they cannot deny access to others, even though the total rent for a year be only one sheep. Thus, the authority of the first tribe is maintained and yet the rights of the people in the second tribe are not abrogated"

Another sheikh raised an issue that has long been a source of trouble. A man from one tribe marries a woman from another tribe with different religious and ethnic beliefs and practices. I issued my pronouncement:

"Let not these principles of division between religions be the basis for dispute between couples. Let the people live together in peace, not dissention. Let the couple decide which faith is the one that values love more than hatred. Too long have the Muslims lived in disunity, fostered by petty jealousy and prejudice."

In another case, the family and religious practices were in question.

"The man was a Baghdadi of noble, orthodox Sunni family. His adventures led to marriage with a Shi'i woman of devout parents from Kabala. After a while, God gave them the glorious gift of a son, who the mother wanted to name Hussein. The product of a lawfully blessed Muslim couple named Hussein can never be received in any manner other than joyfully."

An outside suitor challenged the priority of betrothal rights between first cousins. The outsider tried to assert his claims of affection as being superior to the family blood relationship. The first cousin didn't want to step aside and give up his right to marry his girl cousin.

"The decision was that both the paternal and maternal families are the same in body and customs. There is no need to doubt the suitability of the couple's union because they are of one background. The groom of the family will treat the bride as a sister and as the mother of his children-- he may not do otherwise. Therefore a man has first claim on his father's brother's daughter."

The issue of a blood payment arose because of an unfortunate incident during the previous year. Two young men quarreled and one of them was killed. The involved families disputed how the matter should be settled. The aggrieved party was entitled to take the life of the offender or of a substitute from the tribe.

"The killer was a popular son of the tribal sheikh and none wanted to turn him over to the aggrieved party for execution. My judgment was based in the tribal laws of Islam and called upon the practices of the Prophet.

I advised the injured party that they could demand the life of the offender but that the Prophet had always practiced mercy when possible. There was no reason to insist upon sacrificing the young offender since the tribe of the offender could afford to pay compensation. The blood-money should be accepted. God is merciful. He will repay kindness a hundred times over."

Another matter came up again. I reiterated the usual verdict--

"A man may be armed when he enters a territory other than his own. This does not mean he is hostile. However, it would be better for him to enter disarmed so as to disclose his peaceful intentions. If he brings in arms he must be prepared to repel assaults from the residents."

Interfaith marriages keep on being a problem. A man married a Jewish girl without evoking any religious procedures. She started giving religious instruction to their son. Is that lawful?

"They are both blest by coming from religious homes that worshipped the one God and His prophets. The particular procedures and rituals in each of their religions are of minor importance compared to the acceptance of the one God. But Muslim indoctrination and training must take precedence over her Judaism, according to the Quran.

When she married a Muslim (non-Jew) she forfeited the obligation to teach her son in the way of the Jews. According to her own laws she gave up her dedication to her religion by not marrying a Jew. The Muslim father has the superior obligation to teach his son.

When she accepted a Muslim husband she agreed that if she should adopt Islam then she would be obliged to give their children instruction in that religion.

"The differences in the two religions should not create difficulties that carry over into the relationship between parents or between child and parent. They should be grateful that their children worship the one true God, whatever name they use for Him. They should instill in their children the need to learn more about God in the two paths so readily available."

The perennial dispute over ownership of stray cattle came up again this year. My ruling was the same as others before me had declared.

"The owners of free-range animals are primarily responsible for identifying the beasts, not the neighbor. The owner should have some form of marking on each animal-- a cut on the hoof, a clip of the ear, or a spot of paint on the wool. It is the owner's responsibility to prove that the animal in question belongs to him. Owners must exercise control over their possessions."

A recurring problem arises from the need to assign authority for the children to one of the parents of a divided marriage,

"Islamic law is clear on assigning care for children. While the child is under six he should be in the mother's care. Training the child becomes the father's responsibility after that. These assignments are what is *permitted*. They are guidelines, not laws as to how the assignments of care *must* be made.

Children form bonds of affection over time that should be taken into consideration. A kindly father or mother will have the child's welfare in mind when enforcing the right to assert parental responsibility.

Although these assignments by law are superior to other considerations, a pious Muslim will have compassion in exercising his rights. Consideration should be given to the affectionate bonds between family members and the needs of the siblings, too.

A distinction must be made between exercising care and taking responsibility. It is often the case that the father leaves the older child in his wife's household under her care. Yet by law he retains full responsibility for the older child and can specify conditions on how the mother cares for him."

When food is stolen it automatically becomes *haraam* (forbidden). But what if the food is the meat from a slaughtered animal that wandered from its home territory? The sheikh of the violated territory may feel that he and his people have a right to eat the stray animal.

If he tries to return the animal to the original owner there might be a big fuss. He can't throw away the carcass because it is a sin to kill an animal and waste it. Wouldn't the food become *halaal* (permitted) under those circumstances?

"The Holy Quran and the customs of the Prophet forbid the eating of stolen food. Man cannot ignore the guidance that was sent to him just for his convenience. The one who killed the animal is obligated to return it to its owner and suffer the consequences. The food then becomes lawful for the owner regardless of what transpired.

The only way that the stolen animal can become lawful for the offender is if the original owner sells or makes a gift of this food to him. It would be haraam to let the carcass decay because Muslims disagree on its ownership."

One miserable bastard was emboldened by the crowd to raise an issue. He never would have brought it up if he were alone with his sheikh. But he, like everybody else, wondered what happened to the annual British payment to each of the seven tribal leaders.

Was the British money spent to improve the community (Not likely!) or did it belong to the tribe members to improve their living? Tribal police beat him into submission. Problems are only postponed by using violence, not solved.

"It's all very well to criticize the government for using unnecessary force but when you do so, pray that it will never fall to you to have to deal with disloyalty and treasonous dissatisfactions. The leader must preserve the integrity of his community above all else. That's when the shit hits the fan."

* * * * *

But Jonathan asked me, "How did we British and the Western allies ever get into this business of acquiring colonies of peasants for subjects? Protecting our interests has become more of a burden than a benefit. I see the burden but where are the benefits? You have the perspective of living in two worlds. Perhaps you can help me understand."

I am always ready to share my ideas and understandings:

"Back in the time of the Crusades there was a serious shortage of European land to give away to loyal followers. The leaders (nobles) needed more land (estates) to barter for the support of their knights in oppressive wars of conquest. It took centuries for the new Christianity to develop a glorious battle banner to hide the true land-grabbing motives of these good Christians.

Although the madness of conquest finally abated, the Europeans managed to retain some cities in the Middle East. Their ancestors still pretend to this day that they have sovereign rights. We in foreign service, work to promote dissention among ethnic groups and their leaders so that the West can provide the overlordship that guarantees peace. We make sure that all will be chaos without us

We made the mistake of educating our vassals but now they have seen behind the door. Now we have ended up with responsibilities all over the world. People expect us to rescue them from their misery and poverty. "You can't keep them back on the farm once they've seen "Gay Paree!"

* * * * *

The crowd thinned out as people left for their homes the day after Ashura. They were at peace. They left behind their miseries and sufferings in the war-torn town that had reenacted Dante's Inferno and the Passion Play rolled into one. May God grant them the peace and comfort that they have earned!

The exit roads were packed. There was no escape from the pandemonium-- Jonathan and I pulled off at the closest café. We took a room for the night to let the traffic to Baghdad subside. That was the night that Jonathan and I shared our deepest secret. We confessed that we had almost run our course as spies; we both wanted out. We were tired of doing the devil's bidding no matter which country's flag he was wrapped in.

At the time I viewed our conversational interchange as so much bullshit, liquor talk. Jonathan said that he wanted to retire from MI6 and pursue a new career as an author. He said, "Your life has been so interesting that

I'd like to write about it, to share it with others." At the time I had no idea that he was serious. Later, I would be shocked when he published his accounts of my adventures in two books: Istanbul's Silent Witness, and Istanbul's Secret Warriors."

THE PROPHET'S SWORD

ABDULLAH was frantic. He rang me up at 6 A.M.; I knew that something big had happened. I braced myself for news of a coup d'etat.

Many times I had visited the Topkapi Museum and entered the Islamic relics room with all reverence. I felt blessed to be given the chance to see the same sword that was wielded by our beloved prophet Mohammed-- the sword that that signified the Kingdom of God on earth. It was unbelievable that anyone would defile his sword, let alone steal it.

Some hungry or evil son-of-a-bitch really had sunk that low! He broke open the glass case and grabbed the sword in his profane hands with the help of an accomplice to watch his back. Then he threw it over the walls of the Topkapi Museum. Perhaps it burned into his palms; I like to think so. That bastard had no understanding of the significance of his actions. His act literally shook up the whole Muslim world.

Abdullah and I captured the confederate the very same day, but not the thief. However the accomplice did tell us where he took the sword to be hidden. It was stored in an Istanbul warehouse owned by an American dealer in art and artefacts.

We could have confiscated the knife right then and there. However, we wanted to play the game a bit longer. We wanted to learn who would be audacious enough to purchase such stolen goods. We hoped to catch a whole covey of quail with one net.

Even more constraining was the announcement by the warehouse owner that the sword was in a vault that would instantly destruct if it were tampered with. It sounded like Hollywood bullshit but we had to be cautious. These criminals had us over a barrel and there was nothing for us to do except wait. Anyhow, we were very curious about who would have the balls to put a price on such a magnificent relic and have the effrontery to put it up for sale.

Abdullah wasn't about to let us Americans get off the hook on this one. The crime was important enough to drag us all into it. I was right up there in front when I had to acknowledge the blame on my American compatriots. The owner of the warehouse was American and he was leading all of us around by the nose. American collectors had the money and may even have instigated the theft.

The world of illicit antiquities is as secret as the world of espionage-- I should be right at home there! The select few knew everything-- the public neither knew nor cared what was going on behind the scenes. It was just as well that the public was kept in the dark. Even we professionals were overwhelmed by the enormity of this particularly heinous theft.

Nonetheless, the important people knew where to place their bids for this incredible artefact. Abdullah was authorized by the Topkapi museum to redeem the knife for a million dollars. The American warehouse owner had dragged our county into this mess so our State Department authorized another million dollars to help get the sword back to the Turkish museum.

The custodian of the sword offered us a buy-back deal a week after the theft. He agreed to be guided by a vote of a committee of respectable buyers that we would assemble to decide who should be allowed to buy the sword.

In turn, the thief, the warehouse owner and the custodian of the sword would have full, worldwide immunity from prosecution for theft or possession. The warehouse owner reminded us that the alternative might be the complete destruction of the object. We were going to have to take out our vengeance on the unimportant confederate that we had captured-- everybody else would be protected.

We had to accept those terms and try to get the artefact back in the hands of responsible people. There really was little choice. Our governments gave their assent and we went ahead and populated the committee.

We developed the following list of committee members along with the size of their purchase offers in millions of dollars:

    5.0 Representative from Saudi Arabia
    2.0 Shi'i mullah from Najaf, Iraq
    1.0 Topkai Museum curator, Istanbul
    4.0 Shi'i mullah from Isfahan
    5.0 Smithsonian Museum curator
    1.0 Cairo Museum curator
    0.0 Ashmolean Museum in Oxford, curator

That provided us with seven people to determine the future of Mohammed's holy sword. The custodian first approved the list of seven committee members. Then he insisted on certain operating rules before agreeing to give up the sword to our choice.

The curator of the Ashmolean Museum in Oxford declined to make an offer, thus leaving us with only six prospective purchasers. The final choice would have to be approved by five or more of the members. This was not an auction so we were under no obligation to sell to the highest offer. The only provision about sale price was that it should not be for less than half a million dollars.

Members expressed three concerns:

First: that it be accessible to the faithful.

Second: that it be secure from theft.

Third: that it be protected from humidity to assure that it would not deteriorate over time.

Buyers were invited to explain to us why they felt they should be chosen and what conditions of custodial care would be used.

The three museum curators emphasized that museums were in the best position to provide visibility, security, and preservation

The Saudi said:

The sword would be kept in the Holy Qa'aba in Mecca, along with other artefacts from the early days of Islam. His argument was that the sword originated in Mecca and belonged there.

The mullahs from Iraq and Iran made their case based upon the importance of retaining the blessing of the artefact by maintaining it in a holy city like Karbala or Isfahan.

The Topkapi curator began by claiming ownership because it had been in possession of the Turkish khalifs for centuries. The committee members rebuked him-- only Mohammed had the right to claim ownership.

The committee ignored ownership claims but did take possession into consideration. The curator switched tactics and argued that only the Turkish government had demonstrated reliability in all respects. The sword was never damaged and had been seen by millions of visitors-- "Let the record speak for itself!"

The committee sold the sword back to the Topkapi Museum for a million dollars. The new owner was the same as the old one. The other contenders were disappointed but admitted that the whole affair had been handled in an effective, gentlemanly fashion.

That very evening Abdullah took the sword from the warehouse and hand-carried it back to the same place in the showcase that it still occupies in the Palace. Go see it next time you are in Istanbul.

The slimy American, who arranged the disposition of the sword continued to do business in the same warehouse. However, business was never the same. Abdullah arranged for a uniformed officer to be stationed 24/7 in front of the door to the street. The thief disappeared, a rich man.

IRAN

ONE of my agents in Tehran was stabbed in his hotel room. It was getting so a respectable spy was no longer safe anymore. This killing made us Americans aware that we needed to reposition ourselves in Iran. On a more personal level, all us Americans wanted to exact vengeance.

The dead agent had the unusual name of Dashiell, but everybody called him "Dasher" because of his eagerness. Dasher had been planted in Iran for more than ten years. His cover was established as being the owner of a bookshop in downtown Tehran. We all liked him but knew that our desire to revenge his killing was inimical to performing our tasks to the benefit of our country.

Iran was becoming *the* hot spot in the Middle East. The Shah had lost the support of the people by maintaining a strongly repressive regime. Even the US was finding it embarrassing to justify supplying him with military equipment to maintain his leadership by force.

Israel was always there, standing beside the boiling pot, crying that the Shah was preparing to attack their brave little country. Every drop of oil extracted by Iran was touted as another threat to the existence of tiny Israel.

The Iranian people were fed up with being misused by everybody. They wanted to develop their country's industrial base to meet their own basic needs. The people didn't want the Shah and his cronies, or anybody else, squandering their resources.

The Shah had used rumors of coup d'etat too often as justifications for terrorizing his subjects. His Palace Guard never hesitated to open fire without mercy on the protesters. These confrontations become weekly occurrences.

The people had turned against the Shah and everybody's life was filled with bitterness and dissent. It reached the point where the once respected head of state became a symbol of derision. His subjects were saying that, "The Shah ordered his soldiers to draw a pint of blood from every resident so that it could be sold to the foreigners."

This was America's friend-- the Shah! Some choice of friends we had-- the insupportable Shah or the mob of protesters clamoring to take over the oil resources. And then, there was Israel, vigorously adding fuel to the fire by threatening to attack the oil fields.

A new leader of his people emerged from this fiery mess. His name was Mossadegh and he swept up what respect and support the Shah had lost. This new de facto ruler had to depend upon Russia for foreign assistance, instead of on America.

We Americans couldn't offer support for a pinko like Mossadegh. His very success led to his failure. He forced us Americans to declare our support for the Shah to make sure that we would control the oil fields. He was prime minister for a very short time but the CIA and MI6 mobilized their secret forces against him and replaced his supporters with friendlier faces.

The citizens were furious-- they lost respect for their government and their hopes were hijacked. They weren't capable of dealing with the technology and subterfuge of the modern world.

Everybody was mad at everybody else in those days when Dasher was stabbed. Probably Mossadegh followers were behind the stabbing. If it wasn't the Iranians, then the Soviets must have killed him. The citizens were at a loss to find a countryman, who could lead them out of their morass. They wanted neither the Shah (Americans) nor the Soviets rescuing them with their unrelenting, sticky fingers.

Bazaar merchants with their practical politics made up a large middle class. They had always been influential in Iranian politics. They would ultimately decide Iran's political destiny but they found themselves with no good alternatives. Since the overthrow of Mossadegh there was no popular leader to extract them from their mess. Whatever took place on the political scene would have to take into consideration that Iran was subject to the will of the middle class. The people respected their educated spokesmen and bided their time to be heard.

* * * * *

The bazaars thronged with pubescent boys, the ones who carry your purchases to your car or even to your home. They were of an age to have recently discovered the physical excitement of sex and its potential for bringing monetary reward. They had yet to learn of the criminal abuse of the special virtues of youth and had not yet suffered much from sexually transmitted disease. They were young and innocent, but that's what made them exciting partners for some lonely men.

We know personal stuff about one another in the exclusive club of espionage. We knew that Dasher had been bringing boys off the street to his hotel room for as long as he had been posted abroad. He started employing them when he was in Paris and continued with this diversion after being posted to Tehran.

The boys were already working the streets when Dasher snatched them up for a little companionship. He paid them well and even gave them small gifts. Occasionally they were able to supply him with information that he needed for an assignment.

He did what the rest of us do-- employ locals on special details as confidential informants. We often used informers to provide information, but we usually skipped the sexual side benefits-- at least with the boys.

The delinquency wasn't altogether the fault of the relatives of these boys. They would have preferred that the kids brought home food money from proper work. I always figured that those who were going to get so moral should first find themselves out on the street struggling to survive.

We spies live lonely lives with little chance for forming normal relationships. We have to actively create situations that provide physical gratification and opportunities for temporary, tender interactions. I'm afraid we don't view our colleagues with very sharp moral standards-- maybe we are too sympathetic.

Dasher's playing around never became an issue before this. At least liaisons with 12-year-old boys were safer than with adult seductresses owned and controlled by our enemies. Dasher did have sexual contacts with female prostitutes too. That might please the moralists among us, but it wasn't reassuring to those of us concerned with security matters.

Everything was becoming too complicated. Now I realized that we would have to examine not only the homosexual contacts but also the heterosexual ones as well. The stabbing probably was not the work of a 12-year-old, street boy.

I would start looking at the female prostitutes first. You may wonder why I didn't begin by looking into the possible complicity of one of the political parties. Right! I was in no hurry to enter the complicated society of Irani politics.

A spy can have experiences that are given to few other men. You have license to practice your evil skills on victims that would bring other men life sentences in prison. You use others to your advantage. You become skilful in living on the edge and capable of accomplishing just about anything. But the one thing you can't do is to think like a normal human being. You live too much with watchfulness and suspicion-- you trust and believe no one.

Normal people see what is going on; us spies see what we *suspect* is happening. I couldn't get outside the box on this stabbing of my agent. The only killer I could envision was a Soviet spy or a disgruntled Mossadegh follower. It would never occur to me that an ordinary person might stab a spy. No self-respecting spy would come up with such an outrageous idea.

It took an agent with less than a year's field experience to suggest that maybe a personal friend had stabbed him. Shit! Why hadn't I thought of that? Because I had gone spy-blind-- you know, you see spies hidden behind every bush. But now that my agent had come up with this untenable theory I would have to follow it in my investigation. Imagine how degrading it would be for an international spy to be stabbed with a kitchen knife by an incompetent friend!

* * * * *

Only the crooked minds at Langley could have come up with such an insidious plan! *A CIA agent would kill our discredited agent and then Washington could blame Moscow for the killing.* Not only would we get rid of an agent gone bad, but also, we could expose what looked like a repulsive crime bringing disgrace on the Soviets.

We could invoke the law of *lex talionus*. That would give us a bonus card-- a license to kill a Soviet spy with impunity, as an act of revenge. The American citizens would eat it up-- they always are eager to take revenge against anybody who isn't an American. The whole "free" world would laud American abhorrence of physical aggression even while we were carrying out an assassination.

* * * * *

I hit the street with a fistful of American dollars-- they are sort of a spy's calling card. They can save you a lot of trouble digging out things, and besides, it's only money-- taxpayer's money, not mine.

Whenever you need information about a hotel guest you skip the defensive manager and go right to the desk clerk-- they are always hungry. Dasher's hotel desk clerk provided me with all I needed to know about Dasher's friend of the night, including how to hook up with her.

I took Dasher's girlfriend back to my hotel the first night out. We stopped on the way to have a cup of coffee and a little friendly foreplay chat. She called herself

Gilda-- I saw the resemblance to the role played by Rita Hayworth in the movie of the same name. She had long red hair, or I should say that her wig had long red hair. She acknowledged being Bulgarian. My answers to her questions were brief and imaginative; I had been lying to people half my life so I was good at it.

We finished with the chitchat and went to my room. Two things I learned long ago were: Take sex whenever it's offered, and, never insult a woman by rejecting her. I did my business and sent her on her way. My evening was a big success in every way.

I asked for my old friend Ali at the Tehran police headquarters. We clasped one another affectionately, drank some chi together, and laughed a lot. Then he put it to me-- "You're here to follow up on the stabbing of your agent, Dasher?" I smiled at him and said, "Yeah, you smart bastard! But work won't keep me from having a fun visit to Tehran." He clasped me around the shoulders and said, "Of course not, my brother, and you are coming home with me now to take our noon meal together."

The next day we got down to business. Ali obtained Gilda's proper name from the Irani immigration department. Then he sent a message to Interpol and requested information on her. It was like shooting ducks in a barrel; the report came back detailing her arrests. She was designated a delinquent for her membership in the Communist Party and protesting against the members of parliament who were anti-communist.

Damn! I had almost missed the obvious relationships: > Soviets > Gilda > Dasher killing. I almost went off sniffing the wrong trail for the whole next week. I was pleased with myself for following the old maxim: "Look closest to home, first."

The following evening I brought Gilda to my hotel room for questioning. I jollied her up a bit on the way up there but then my demeanor changed once I locked the door behind us. I paid her up front to keep her as friendly as I could under those circumstances. Then I explained that instead of sex I wanted some answers about her client, Dasher.

She became defensive immediately. I wouldn't have believed her if she were otherwise. She responded with an alibi, "I was on a job with my friend Olga the day he was stabbed. I heard about it the next morning but I hadn't seen him for a week. You can ask Olga about it."

I didn't want Gilda to have a chance to prompt Olga about the alibi so I called in one of my agents to help me. He kept Gilda locked in the room while I went out to find and question Olga. All it cost me was a cup of coffee to get Olga to confirm the details of their joint assignment the night Dasher was killed.

Gilda had looked like one swell prospect but she took me nowhere. What next? I had no suspect and no leads. All I had was the inculcated suspicion that everything was the fault of the Soviets. I was wrong.

My suspicion that a Soviet spy killed Dasher had a big flaw in it-- spies don't kill enemy spies. We are not kids with BB guns shooting at sparrows! It violates the fundamental principle in the spy code of ethics. "Spies should never regard a counterpart, employed by the enemy, as a personal enemy. They should show mutual respect if they happen to meet unintentionally, when not occupied professionally."

I knew Gilda was in Dasher's room the day of the murder. Was anybody else there, too? Oh, yes! The murderer. Perhaps Dasher had a regular, little friend from the bazaar, who did various tasks for him. The clerk would know of such a person and where he could be located.

I went down to the desk and politely asked the clerk to accompany me. We went to a cleaning closet where we wouldn't be disturbed. He realized I was serious because these days the only foreigners in the hotel were spies. He knew enough to mind his own business unless he was confronted with force. These weren't like the good old days of leisure and pleasure. People were serious these days; he cracked wide open.

"Yes, Mr. Dasher had a bum boy, who waited in the cloak room of the hotel to be summoned. The boy's nickname is Teddi. He works as a porter in the market."

While I had the clerk pinned down I asked him, "Who went into Mr. Dasher's room the day of his death?" The clerk knew that this was valuable information and was reluctant to give it away for free. He looked at me pleadingly and I understood. I peeled off a couple of good-sized bills and his mouth wagged automatically.

"Gilda was up there for about an hour. After that, Mr. Dasher sent for Teddi to come up to his room. He must have sent Teddi on an errand because he was only there long enough to get his orders for the day." I brushed off the shoulder of his jacket reassuringly with my hand, just like Humphrey Bogart does in the movies. I told him, "Send Teddi to my room."

An hour later there was a timid knock on the door. I opened it carefully and pulled Teddi inside quickly. I was trying to make him nervous and talkative. I asked him about the day of the murder. He pleaded that he knew nothing about it. "What murder?" I ruffed him up a bit and tried again.

"I only did what Mr. Dasher told me to do. He said I should keep watch in the lobby and see if an English-speaking stranger came to the desk. I was supposed to rush up to his room and tell him if one did show up."

"So?" With my urging Teddi continued, "A man came into the hotel and went upstairs. I waited about ten minutes after the stranger left and then I went up to Mr. Dasher's room. He was lying on the floor holding his belly. He said that the visitor had stabbed him and I should go downstairs and get help."

I speared him with my eyes, "So?" He started again, "Well, I was afraid and didn't want to get mixed up in something like that so I ran back to the bazaar and continued my work there as usual. The next day word got around that an American from the hotel had died suddenly."

Little Teddi was too gentle a soul to have killed Dasher. The murderer must have been the visitor. I had to learn his identity. I went back to interrogate the desk clerk some more. What a surprise-- "He was feeling sick and was not expected back until tomorrow." I spent the remainder of the day going through the police records of the hotel employees.

The next day began with a glorious sunrise that matched my mood. I was at the reception desk when the clerk arrived. The only thing he added to what he had already told me was that the guest spoke like an American. Nobody else in the hotel seemed to know anything about this American friend.

I asked the clerk to bring Teddi to me. Teddi said he didn't know anything more than he already told me. But I could see that Teddi was uncomfortable-- he was holding back something. Good interrogation depends upon knowing how to use timing. I had been gentle with Teddi but now I put him in a vice.

He confessed that he had seen the strange visitor once before in Dasher's room a month or so earlier. They visited like they were good friends. Dasher sent Teddi out for a bottle of araq (distilled liquor) to drink and when he returned they were still chatting away in English.

"They didn't suppose that I know any English. I don't know much but I understood some of their conversation. The stranger seemed to know all about Mr. Dasher's work and they mentioned the CIA and the 'Company' several times. I had no doubt but that they were both American spies. I kept quiet.

After that experience I wanted to stay away from Mr. Dasher and his spy friend. I tried to avoid him but he sent for me repeatedly and I didn't want to become conspicuous or get him mad at me. I went back to him several times for his pleasure but not to run his errands like before."

The phrase, "An American spy, you say?" bounced around in my head. On a hunch I went to my office to retrieve some personnel folders to use as a sort of line-up. The desk clerk and Teddi both recognized one of my agents as Dasher's mysterious American friend. I returned to the office with a heavy heart.

I summoned my agent and confronted him with the evidence. I accused him of murdering Dasher. He stopped me cold, "I did it on orders from Langley." Then it came out-- those bastards at the Central Office went over my head again and used one of my own staff to conduct this despicable operation.

They ordered my agent to kill his brother-agent, Dasher. A pencil pusher in the State Department dreamt up this nefarious operation. It was illegal, improper, and indecent.

Agent Dasher had proved untrustworthy by stealing two million dollars. He had to be removed permanently, and no one would be in a better position to do the deed than a fellow agent. The assignment was made and carried out. All I could do was sit back and fume. If I made too much noise I might find myself in the same circumstances as Dasher.

CHOLERA

I HAD just arrived at the offices of the World Health Organization when two people rushed me from both sides and pinned me to a desk. I could hardly twist my head. As I swivelled around I felt the sharp, stinging pain of a needle in my arm.

I looked up at them helplessly. I was a victim of a joke. I would be leaving the next day to go to the Far East so I needed the Cholera vaccination. My colleagues just decided to make a fun game out of it.

At about this time every year I came to Geneva, Switzerland to review the progress of the annual cholera epidemic. The cholera would always start in Pakistan or China and travel westward along the Silk Road. Rarely did it begin in China and only one time did it start in an entirely different county.

The World Health Organization carefully followed the spread of this disease. They supervised precautionary measures taken in the field, usually relating to sources of drinking water. They would struggle with the bug all through the hot-wet season and then the cases of infection would drop back to a lower level. Thousands of people died miserably every year. WHO did their best but it was only a holding action.

The CIA had two special interests in this annual, public-health event. First, we watched closely the starting place and movement of the infection. Secondly, we compared this year's path with the patterns of previous years. Why? Because cholera could be used as a very destructive weapon.

At the same time, we in the CIA were actively using a poison that simulated the symptoms of cholera. We had to remain vigilant because our enemies might start using the poison too. We could infect a victim and induce such a massive response that he died within twenty-four hours without realizing that he had been poisoned. When everybody around was dying of cholera we didn't have to hide any bodies or account to anybody for possible poisonings. The poison was just too good to be true. Soon, others would get their hands on it.

Such deaths may have seemed natural, even though suspicious. Even important people just suddenly dropped out of the political scene with a minimum of fuss. Think back to Iran's Prime Minister Mossadegh, who led the revolt against Britain. Then the most famous of all was Yasser Arafat, the Representative of the PLO. With just a poof he was gone from the scene. King Farouk of Egypt faded out quietly.

The Shah disappeared from the game when he became a liability for us. There were many others of lesser importance. Sometimes we had to liquidate some of our own people by sending them out into the field and bringing their corpses back flanked by honor-guards. It's a cruel world out there!

The cholera season started off as usual. There was nothing strange about the path of the spreading epidemic. That picture three years earlier was very different from the current one. At that time, the first cases were found in Western Mongolia, a thousand miles north of the normal tropical origin of past years. Then progression was slowly to the west, unlike other years when the region to the south was blanketed with cases. That year we watched the spread of disease through the northern Caucuses and into the Soviet Central Asian Republics. By the end of that season the Republics had been devastated. The Ukraine was largely spared but little Chechnya was almost obliterated.

Hum? I wonder who could have had it in for a quarrelsome Chechnya? It was incredible that Russia would disburse cholera to produce genocide of that magnitude but there was no other explanation unless you were a believer in the Vengeance of the Lord. We wanted to warn the world of the danger, but had nothing to prove whose hand had spread the evil seed.

We would love to have been able to expose the Soviet enemy as the perpetrator of that crime. The Russians were always accusing America of committing international crimes. They constantly reminded the world that it was American bombs that killed hundreds of thousands of civilians in Hiroshima and Nagasaki.

We finally had something equally abhorrent against Russia but couldn't prove it. No one would believe such a wild accusation. That was three years ago and now we had lost our opportunity to use the disease as a propaganda weapon against them. All we could do was watch the current, annual pattern and be ready to send out international warnings without attributing blame.

Langley had scheduled a CIA agent and three political figures to join the cholera dance of death. The CIA agent, who had to be eliminated, was under my command and we had known each other for about five years. Langley decided, "He has to go."

I couldn't sign his death warrant. I'm hard-hearted enough to be able to kill in the course of my work but I couldn't kill one of my own in cold blood-- well maybe I could if my own life depended upon it. It would be just as well not to put me to the test.

Maybe I shouldn't tell you my agent's name. They say, "Don't give it a name if you're going to kill it." Allen was an OK guy. He was approaching retirement age and he hoped to increase his resources by a little fast shuffling. He stole two million dollars instead of delivering it to one of our clients in the Persian Gulf. He screwed up so badly that he didn't even get to keep the loot.

You might very well say, "So what! Is that any reason to have him killed?" But it placed Langley in a quandary about what to do with Allan. He could no longer be trusted to do the work of a CIA agent. If they fired him he wouldn't have enough pension to live on and he would be pissed at the CIA. You can't just let hungry, ex-agents walk around on the streets, especially if they hate the Agency; they know too much.

Allan was sent to Pakistan with a message and a mission. He may have suspected he was being set up, but I hope not. He ended up in a mass grave for those who fell to cholera. He may not have been given a proper Christian burial but at least he avoided a dishonourable discharge.

All this put me to thinking about my own retirement. Perhaps I should say, "worrying" about my retirement because getting out of the CIA is not so easy. I said a little prayer for Allan. He was a friend and still had my respect despite his malfeasance.

The cholera-like death could only be used effectively in an infected region. Two remaining targets were outside the cholera region so we had to send them to Pakistan. We staged a conference on Islamic Institutions in Eastern Asia and invited a few participants from outside Pakistan to broaden the point-of-view.

It was all bullshit like most conferences, but nobody realized that it was a set-up. Both of our intended victims attended. The subject of the conference was, "The Role of Government in a Muslim Country."

The conference was disrupted when those two participants came down with cholera. The variety was extremely virulent and the two gentlemen died very quickly. The conference was closed for health reasons.

I was ordered to see that the one remaining target was dispatched promptly. He was a bold Christian Arab named George, who was attracting too many followers, as far as the West was concerned. He introduced a new level of violence into Palestinian politics. The suicide bombing level increased markedly and everybody was talking about martyrdom. We found him inconvenient and knew that sooner or later we would have a major collision.

My staff and I studied George and his living circumstances. We failed to find a way to assassinate him and still avoid blame. The whole world would still suspect us even if we secretly silenced the guy. We had waited too long. We let this weed grow too strong and tall. If we killed George he would become a martyr and the Palestinian movement would surge.

I returned to my Istanbul office and awaited new instructions. Finally the State Department decided to follow my recommendation-- "Let George die a natural death of old age."

REVOLUTION IN IRAQ

THAT day in 1958 began like any other day but sure finished unlike any other. I was sitting in a gazebo playing a game of chess and exchanging information and ideas with Nuri Said. He was a very interesting man.

Nuri was Prime Minister of Iraq and had been its *de facto* ruler since the birth of Iraq in the days after WWI. Nuri was a statesman in the full sense. He was right up there with the best-- Churchill and Gamal Abdul Nasser. Truly great statesmen led their countries from behind a desk rather than by waving at the people from a limousine as they ride by in magnificent parades.

These powerful figures are the prime ministers are the CEO's who run the government. They are appreciated for their skills and mastery. You might very well admire them without liking them; they often are unscrupulous. They develop effective policies to guide their nation's destiny, although you might be appalled at their occasional unscrupulousness.

A statesman is so effective that you have to respect him even though he is your enemy. In any foreign service like spying, you can find yourself admiring the adversary you are dedicated to defeat. Nuri Said was British-educated and trained. He was bright and cultured, quite unlike most Arabs I dealt with. I liked him personally.

Nuri had always controlled Iraq with a strong hand and full British backing. The people used to joke, "Iraq's most important government office is in London at Number 10 Downing Street."

Nuri was becoming more and more dependent on the British during my tenure as America's head spy for the Middle East. At the same time he was trying to avoid being seen in British company-- it was enough that he was known for being "in their pocket." The more Nuri became dependent on Britain, the more distant they had to appear in public.

Several major events signaled the winding down of the old colonial empire in the Middle East during the few years of my tenure as head spy Nasser and fellow officers converted the Egyptian monarchy into a people's republic. Emerging Arab nationalism had been suppressed for so long that it broke through with a fury.

A short time later Egypt and Syria formed a confederated government to confront the West. The Arabs finally were uniting against imperialist England. Before anyone could adjust to those new realities, Egypt nationalized the Suez Canal.

Israel and Britain saw the chance to weaken Arab nationalist progress by attacking Egypt. France joined in to support Israel's simultaneous land grab. The pretence for military intervention was to restore the canal to its historical owners-- Britain and France.

This point in time was a watershed in American intervention in Middle Eastern politics. It was when the United States publicly condemned the military actions of its European allies. That diplomatic action openly acknowledged the American withdrawal of support for British colonialism and a dedication to American interests.

Nuri saw that it would be anathema for Iraq to continue her dependence on Britain and her colonial policies. After a lifetime of mutual support it was too late for an amicable divorce. Britain was on the way out and America was the new king-of-the-mountain.

Syria quarreled with Egypt and was afraid of her more powerful partner. The imperialist West saw the opportunity to make one last stand to counter the Arab nationalism, so they prepared to attack the new federation from inside Jordan.

The Anglo-Iraqi-Jordanian schemers announced the formation of a union of Jordan with Iraq. It was an alliance of the pro-western Arab rulers. The new union was supposed to be a counterbalance to the emerging nationalism of the Arabs, but instead it fanned the flames of revolution. Once again the West had infuriated the Arabs.

During a brief swing of the pendulum, the Iraqi opposition government was able to dispatch troops to the border of Lebanon in support of Arab Nationalism. The Arabs prevented the Western powers from invading Lebanon and spreading their control with their new pseudo-Arabism.

Nuri made his final mistake when he sent troops to fight alongside the British to put down nationalist insurrection in Jordan. He incurred the wrath of the Palestinian refugees in Jordan who turned against their monarch, King Hussein. The Iraqi officers refused to obey Nuri's orders; that's where my story of the revolution begins. It was a bad day for all. The insurgent officers returned to Baghdad.

* * * * *

Nuri and I moved closer politically as he withdrew from public association with the Brits. He never gave up his old friends; he just softened his Anglophile appearance. He wanted inside information that I would have obtained routinely. He invited me to visit him at his office in the royal palace because he wanted to use me.

Nuri spoke flawless Turkish from his early years of service in the Turkish army. We enjoyed conversing in Turkish and we both loved the game of chess. Need I remind you that I lived in Turkey for the first 20 years of my life?

That was the beginning of a strange, brief friendship. He apologized for not receiving me properly in his office. He explained, "I now use my office mostly for disinformation. I make sure that the spies know all about what goes on there and whom I see."

He kept the breakfast hour open for our weekly visit. He confided that lately he had more time to spend in pleasurable pursuits because the political situation was no longer in his hands to control. When we visited we talked about how America might be able to slide in to take over a lot of the functions being performed by Britain. But most of the time we just played chess.

A statesman like Nuri is a natural-born chess player. He is quite unlike the blustery politician whose main function is to serve as a front for the party. Chess players and statesmen work out their moves intelligently and dispassionately. They anticipate the countermoves and are prepared with their own responses. There are few surprises as play proceeds. Actions and reactions are always carefully selected to lead to the final goal. Losses result from weaknesses, not because of carelessness or poor judgment.

I wanted to have faith in my friend, Nuri, but 95% of Iraq's oil was pledged away to British companies. What could I think except that he had given away the wealth of his country? As an American employee I had a responsibility to further British interests when they corresponded to American interests, but it wasn't my job to keep the British in control.

Surly, the assignment of Iraqi resources to British companies was against my country's interests. I should work to open a chink in the agreements that Nuri had made with Britain, and create opportunities for the Americans. My conscience told me that I should do what I could to work against the British. For once I was thinking with the dedication of an American foreign service employee.

I asked Nuri if he believed that his pro British policies had benefited the Iraqis. He replied, "Of course, no small country can stand up against the world on its own. A more intelligent question would be, 'Nuri, would you have been wiser to have selected Russia or France to provide a personal model?' "

He continued, "Personally, I have always admired the Britishness of Winston Churchill-- he has been my model. I could never have taken a simpering Frenchman or a vulgar Stalin as a model."

I asked him what he really thought about the establishment of Israel on Arab land. He grunted and scowled, "It is an abomination for us Arabs but a godsend for those of us, who are trying to control the Arabs to our advantage. Israel is a *Weapon of Mass Disruption.*"

Nuri's detractors accused him of having Jewish roots. I wanted to ask him if that were true, but I didn't have the *chutzpah*. I asked him what he thought of the

Israelis. He just spit and refused to follow that direction of the conversation. He rebuked me, "Let's get back to playing chess!"

I'm a nervy bastard! I asked him something that only an intimate friend should ever dare ask. "How will you be judged when you stand before God?" He replied, "I am my own hardest critic. I have dealt too severely with others in order to achieve goals that may have been wrong. If I had my life to live over again I would be an Arab nationalist and a proud one. As I stand before God I will not be able to declare that I am exactly proud of the life I lived."

That took me down an old, familiar path. How many times have I asked myself, "Are you doing what is expected by your employer or are you doing what is good? Are you really making this a better world?" If you are inclined to ask questions like that then you probably shouldn't be a spy.

* * * * *

Nuri had uncanny powers! That very morning of our last visit he told me, "I have enjoyed our visits very much. I'm afraid there will not be many more of them." My God! He not only controlled the destinies of the world but he could forecast the future, too!

We were setting up our chess pieces for a new game in the gazebo on the front lawn of the palace. We took a few sips of bitter Arabic coffee and were just settling down when we heard an unexpected sound in the distance.

Slowly the rumble increased until it took on the inescapable sound of tanks being brought up to surround the palace. Nuri took out his automatic pistol and jacked up a shell into the chamber and then put it back in his shoulder holster. We waited.

The tanks stopped several hundred yards from the front of the palace and opened fire. The artillery struck the roof and the palace façade. No one entered or left by the front entrance that was in clear view. Salvos from several tanks penetrated the entranceway; smoke broke out in the inner courtyard.

We kept quiet and waited in the gazebo on the front lawn. There was a frightening silence. Some minutes later, automatic weapons opened up with several bursts of ominous fire. We waited quietly hoping that none of the attacking army had spotted us; we were alone and deserted. Did I mention that we were scared shitless, too?

We had no way of knowing at the time that the death of the monarchy and the birth of the People's Republic had just been proclaimed. The automatic weapon fire in the rear of the palace announced the execution of all the royal family and personal servants. Nuri was the only person in the inner government still left alive.

Several officers arrived and went through the front entrance. The tanks had done their noisy job and were retired to the outer walls of the palatial grounds. We still remained silent. Destiny had placed Nuri in my hands. I could call out and betray him or I could continue to hide with him and then help him escape.

In the eyes of many, Nuri had held back the advancement of Iraq. He gave away Iraq's natural resources and had done little to build a nation. He made Iraq's sovereignty a joke, and destroyed the lives of many protesting citizens. Wouldn't the world praise me if I pushed him out of the gazebo and into the open to be shot down like a dog?

I answered my own question. "Probably not, because I would end up a bloody mess alongside him!" The people would be vindictive and in no temper to sit around and exonerate the innocents. It was not a time to debate loyalties, it was time to make our escape.

Besides, I was obligated as an American agent to assist Britain, our main ally in the Middle East. I wasn't paid to formulate or debate policy; I was paid to go into action. After an hour the tanks retreated further toward the city to secure the access road to the palace. Most of the officers and troops left. They were deployed to take up stations at the ministries, the transportation centers, the newspaper offices, and the communication centers.

Our chances of escaping would diminish the longer we waited for order to be restored. It was then or never. We walked slowly over to the American Embassy car and Nuri entered the rear while I put on the driver's cap and positioned myself in the chauffeur's seat. Then we started on the frightening gauntlet to town.

Nobody tried to stop us as we left the entrance to the palace; we held our breath and continued. We realized that the officers in charge did not realize that anyone of importance had been left alive. They thought that there was no need to establish checkpoints to prevent people from leaving the palace-- in the excitement they forgot all about Nuri. The manned checkpoints had orders to stop only unauthorized entry into the palace to prevent looting.

We encountered only one checkpoint along the road to the city. As we approached it I noted that the soldiers only had light arms. We could have crashed our way through the barricade if necessary, but that would have initiated a terrible hullabaloo. We kept our cool and I casually advised the guard that I was conveying the American Ambassador to his residence.

I asked Nuri where I should take him. He said that he could trust only his family but he didn't want to put them in danger. He said, "Once again in my life I feel like a street dog with no place to go." As we drove along into town I couldn't help wondering if the world would thank me for rescuing Nuri. He was a strong man and an even stronger enemy. Now he felt vulnerable and had self-doubts, so uncharacteristic for him.

He said, "I have faced danger many times without flinching but certain death is not so easy." We review our life when faced with death. Nuri was a "strong" leader, a statesman and a policymaker, but he was human, also.

* * * * *

Nuri's policies were anachronistic. Why is it that all people think that the political principles, so useful at one stage of a country's development, are equally useful at a later one? Perhaps it stems from our belief in God. He is eternal and infallible. He transfers these holy blessings to His regents on earth so they supposedly take on the same imperishable qualities as God, Himself. We acknowledge these celestial qualities as in the phrase, "Your Holy Majesty!"

Family is the basic social unit. Cooperation within the family is necessary for survival in the primitive stages of society. You can call it what you like but it is rudimentary socialism. When that society becomes wealthy enough to work out bartering with neighbors it is functioning with a form of socialist economy. A community investment in infrastructure is needed for a society when it becomes a large group of impoverished peasants with no upper class. The aggregation of capital for creating infrastructure has to be delegated to the communist government.

Communism and socialism would seem to be the early mechanisms for building the infrastructure of a society. Supply and demand can take over to regulate industry once industry is established. Then socialism and communism will be discarded.

This would seem to be a natural political progression. In addition, an impartial justice system must provide protection from government suppression of dissent. Lastly, excessive accumulation of wealth and power in a few hands needs to be prevented.

* * * * *

It would have been foolish for me to drop Nuri off at the family home. By now the rebels would be searching for him and his house would be the first place they would look for him. Nuri must have walked a block or so from where I dropped him off. From what I learned later, he went to a friend of the family who made it possible for him to make his farewells. They provided him with food and clothing and he started out alone so as not to attract attention.

What a comedown for a statesman of his caliber! He knew what it was like to be a fugitive citizen-- he had created many of them before. He hoped he might remain undetected and travel by common vehicles to the port city of Basra in southern Iraq. Once there, he would be able to reach Kuwait or even go along further south to Abu Dhabi. His trip into exile could be a long and painful one-- but it wasn't.

Nuri was captured at a checkpoint as he left Baghdad. The guards who recognized him were drunk with the wine of liberation. They shared their excitement with anybody within hearing distance. The mob crowded around to see the captured animal. They were delighted that his true nature was finally exposed-- he wore a woman's gown for a disguise. Nothing could please the crowd more than seeing this powerful man brought down to their common level.

They could revile him from a distance but they had to come closer to be able to spit on him. Those closest to him couldn't resist pounding on this helpless man. They killed him then and there with their bare hands-- they tore him to pieces.

Later, when I learned of his capture I thought-- I'm made of flesh and blood but I'm not an "animal." Thank God I was spared the spectacle of watching man's inhumanity to man. You may think that we spies are heartless and get accustomed to atrocious deaths-- we don't. We were born to loving mothers just like you were.

After a few minutes, nothing was left but a bloody corpse. People closed in on the scene from all directions-- just like ants assembling to eat the remains of a dead animal. The people stripped off pieces of his clothing for souvenirs of the glorious occasion. Before long, not a stitch of clothing covered the corpse. Nuri was converted to a mass of garbage.

He was unrecognizable, but that was not enough. Too long the public had suffered from his repressive bullies; too many families had been destroyed by his orders. The people rejoiced as they hacked his body to pieces. The remains were crushed under the tires of army vehicles driven by frenzied men.

The main bloody mess was hung outside the wall of the Ministry of Defense to dry in the sun. It's hard to say which enjoyed the disgusting spectacle most-- the frenzied crowd or the swarms of flies. What was God doing in the meantime, laughing or crying?

* * * * *

I had broken one of the primary rules of successful fieldwork, "Avoid establishing patterns in your routines." I became known as an associate of Nuri and those spying on him knew when I visited and knew that it was I who helped him escape.

I felt that I had become useless as a spy for the Americans. It was then that I had the ridiculous thought of quitting the Americans and offering my services to the Turkish government. But my immediate problem was to stay alive so I didn't ponder much about the future. I just ran! While Nuri chose to flee south I elected to go north and was more successful than he was, thanks to God!

There is a small window for escaping from the new authorities after a coup d'etat. It's before the new managers and officers receive orders from their superiors. Reorganizing the institutions takes a little time if the government just changed. That's when the window of escape can open. Given time, the list of wanted fugitives lengthens and escaping from the country becomes harder. The trick is to escape before the net tightens and the guards start looking for you.

Since I was on the run I couldn't take any of the usual, comfortable means of transportation. I had to use beat-up, old, inter-city shared taxis and vans. My plan was to go to northern Iraq and from there go to southern Turkey. Once I was safe in Turkey I would be able to take a first-class bus to Istanbul.

So that's how I ended up in one of the cities in northern Iraq, called Kirkuk. There is a certain inherent safety in a city because of community barriers between ethnic groups. A sort of a firewall grows naturally between ethnic districts. Communication is highest within the neighborhood but poorest between people from different districts. Kirkuk has some distinct ethnic groups so I had some protection from being discovered.

When I stopped over for the night I had a chance to think about how lucky I was to have escaped from Baghdad. Baghdad was becoming too large a metropolis. I realized that we needed to move our Iraq base to Kirkuk because there was such turmoil in Baghdad, A local informant and I looked at some Kirkuk property for sale that could serve as our new office.

Nobody stopped me en route to Turkey, where I took the first comfortable bus I dared use. It took two nights for us to travel all the way across Anatolia to Istanbul. I went to my Uncle Ramses' Star Residence for a pampered two-day recovery break. I deserved it.

INCIRLIK AIRBASE

IT WAS a horrible time for an assassination-- as if there ever is a good time. The nationalism broiling in the Middle East provided a backdrop for the elimination of a figure that stood for American strength-- the Commander for the American Air force based in Turkey. His death only exposed the difficulties of squatting in a weakly committed country like Turkey.

The killing of an American major stationed in Turkey would be an embarrassment to both countries. The Americans would be obliged to demand a public explanation to mollify their voters. At the same time, the Turkish Prime Minister would have to take a stand for justice, yet not be seen as coddling the foreigners based in his country. The mess called for rolling out the big guns so our State Department sent me to Incirlik.

It seemed to me as if this investigation would be right down lieutenant Abdullah's alley. In fact the two of us should be working on this case together. I phoned him. He said, "You just caught me as I was going out the door. I was planning to fly out to Incirlik to investigate the murder."

I asked him, "What makes you think the major was murdered?" He replied, "His orderly found a pool of vomit in his bed that had a peculiar smell. Do you want to come and take a look for yourself?" I answered excitedly, "Hold the plane. I'm on my way."

This was one assignment that we both were going to take seriously. No doubt the Turkish Prime Minister was already alerted and alarmed about the possible consequences. He was the main functionary in maintaining the delicate balance between the government and its citizens. If he mishandled the situation he could be faced with public demonstrations and even riots. Hell! It was only a few years ago that they hanged their own prime minister!

Abdullah had the foresight to bring a top forensic physician along with us. The medical angle would have to be handled by a non-politicized expert. The whole world would be waiting for the medical report's cause of death.

Abdullah also brought along a military advocate to monitor our investigation. He would assure the world that everything was being done properly during the investigation.

The Vice Commander in charge of the airbase was Captain Perry and he personally Jeeped out onto the runway to meet our plane. He was demonstrating to us that those men stationed on the base were giving this incident the importance it merited.

As we flew to Incirlic, Abdullah and I commiserated with each other about being in the hot seat. Both our governments would be after us to come up with a miraculous solution that would make both sides look angelic to their own people. Perhaps we would be able to blame the killing on a Russian.

So all we had to do was turn up a plausible suspect and help our respective employers put a favorable spin on the whole mess. You are asking, "Were we ready to fabricate the facts to help our countries save face?" The answer is a resounding, "Hell, yes! That's what we get paid for." I no longer was an investigator; I was working for the CIA.

We wanted a quick summary about the possible crime from the Acting Commander so we wouldn't lose time getting started. The detailed report could wait.

"A local Turkish woman, who had spent the night with Major Orwell, awoke to find him dead in bed. She noted that he was cold to her touch and he appeared to have stopped breathing. She said that there was a pool of vomit on his side of the bed.

The previous evening they dined together in the officer's mess and then retired. She didn't notice anything unusual during the meal or afterward.

After waking up and finding him dead she dressed and then called his orderly. The orderly reported the matter to the Officer of the Day and guards were placed about the bedroom and the dining room to protect evidence. Unfortunately the alarm was not raised until after the cook had started mucking about preparing breakfast. The woman was placed in custody as a witness."

The Vice Commander of the base took charge of the scene. All required security measures were taken over by his aide de camp. He was supposed to "lock the barn door" now that the horse had escaped!

The nude body of Major Orwell was still lying in the bed. His head was on one pillow and beside him was the other pillow with the impression from another head. His body showed no obvious signs of trauma.

The medical officer remarked that he found it peculiar that the woman had slept through the noise and stench of the Major's vomiting. She responded by saying that she was a very sound sleeper. Perhaps he died of indigestion or a heart attack?

The assassin chose to use a rather slow-acting poison. He played it safe-- by the time the alarm was raised he was long gone. He was not a suicide bomber or a reckless patriot with a martyr complex. This was an open challenge for us to capture the killer.

But my enthusiasm put the horse before the cart. Before investigating a murder you should be sure you have one. I urged the forensic doctor to begin his investigation immediately and to keep us informed about anything supporting murder as the cause of death. I asked him to be on the watch for poisoning, in particular. By evening the M.D. had opened the corpse to get access to the vital organs. Just before bedtime he summoned Abdullah and me.

We found him in a treatment room up to his elbows in his dirty task. "I just thought I'd give you some advance information. The appearance of the liver, both in color and size, indicates a massive attempt to reject an ingested poison. I could guess which poison was administered but would prefer to await toxicology lab reports before being too specific."

We thanked him for his help, "That's what we were waiting to hear!" It was time to go into motion. I knew before we began that I would get the usual evasive answers and even downright lies. My shrug of despair was countered by Abdullah's reassuring smile, "We'll get the bastard!"

You may wonder why I have to depend upon disloyal informants and witnesses. The answer is obvious-- Middle East nationals behave in a compliant manner but underneath they are loyal to their own. They usually hate their masters, to whom they are obligated. The Turks are even more anti-West than the Arabs.

The Arabs are children. They joined in the games with the Brits but never realized just how much the Brits were taking advantage of them. The Turks are shrewd and worldlier than the Arabs.

Interrogation might yield misleading results but could produce leads to investigate. It didn't. The results of the interrogation were as fruitless as expected. We asked leading questions of our subjects without sharing with them our reasons for asking them. We got the dumb answers we deserved.

We started our questioning with the cook. He never left the kitchen during the major's evening meal. He was the least likely one on our list to be involved because he couldn't have controlled the distribution of the poisoned food. We had to move along to the waiter who served the food.

The waiter recounted his service for the previous evening. He admitted to nothing and gave us no reason to doubt his veracity. Just as we were dismissing him he addressed us, "If you please, there was an irregularity in our meal for that evening. The major loved rice pudding and I served it to him that evening. Usually he disposed of the pudding at the table but that time he had me bring it to his room."

The cook confirmed that the orderly *cum* waiter had served up the rice pudding in the bedroom occupied by the major and his lady friend. I reviewed our notes relating to the scene. There was no mention of finding a dish of rice pudding in the bedroom. What could have happened to it?

We re-questioned the orderly. He recalled bringing the pudding to the bedroom but he knew nothing about its disposal. He swore that the major was still awake and alert when he left him for the last time.

The next day we brought the shackled orderly in for questioning. We had minimal circumstantial evidence of his complicity but we needed to appear to be making progress in this important case. That move proved to be a mistake. The press outside the base was waiting for just such a development to maintain public interest.

We had to go on the defensive and deny that the orderly had been arrested. We mumbled, "The investigation is ongoing and we will apprise you of any new developments." The press did the only thing they could be expected to do-- focus on the prime suspect.

The Turkish newspaper editorials praised, "Those Turks, who defend our homeland from the foreign devils." The waiter couldn't resist playing the national hero role. He cried for his abused Nation in every news and TV interview. Within a week he was a national hero. Everybody turned to the news section before going to the daily soccer results.

The public confession of the waiter was sufficient to get an indictment against him, but then our case fell apart. The cook came forward and claimed that he poisoned the American major for nationalist reasons. He declared that the waiter had stolen the operation from him and that the waiter had nothing to do with the assassination.

The cook vaulted into the TV and news stations to become the new defender of the nation. Nobody would be crazy enough to try to indict a national hero like him. With the heroic cook confessing to the same crime we had to back off. We didn't dare push for an indictment against either the waiter or the cook. We were stymied.

Both claimed to be the true hero of the Republic. The media couldn't decide which was the national hero so they applauded them both.

We didn't know who had committed the murder and we had no idea of how to proceed to satisfy the citizenry. Thank God for Abdullah. He had been rather quiet during our investigation, but he had been thinking. He remembered that the girlfriend mentioned that a bowl of rice pudding had been a part of the crime scene. What happened to it?

We searched the premises and found a bowl in a service sink that was half-washed. We took it to our forensic physician to verify its contents. He affirmed that it contained enough deadly poison to kill ten men.

At that point I paused to think, "Does it really mattered who killed the major? The media have not just one, but two national heroes. Who could want more? But I'm an investigator and not one to walk away from a judicial quandary. Somebody killed the major and I was going to find out who did it!

The forensic lab identified the fingerprints on the pudding dish as belonging to the major's lady. When confronted with this evidence she confessed. She told us that Turkish nationalists had approached her and offered her $10,000 to poison the major. None of us pushed too hard to find out who the accessories to the murder were. The truth is that we didn't want to know. If we knew their identity we would be forced to take legal action and nobody wanted to prosecute Turkish patriots.

That night Abdullah and I drank a bottle and a half of raku in an attempt to deal with the conflicting allegiances that filled our breasts. We acknowledged that the reports we sent our superiors should contain what they wanted to hear.

Nobody wanted to know that a mere woman was paid to poison the "American King of Incirlik." It sounded better to accuse, "Misguided Turkish soldiers, who out of irrepressible loyalty to their country, avenged a century of exploitation" And that, "The American, Major Orwell died in the line of duty."

It took a lot of money to arrange the truths that the public wanted to hear. The lady went to live in Anatolia with a promise that if she ever surfaced again she would be quickly "disappeared." A generous stipend made it unnecessary for her to ever resurface.

The cook and waiter were invited to take early discharges and to do so quietly. Should they reappear they would be prosecuted for murder, but they might encounter revenge and never make it to trial. Another $100,000,00 bought their full cooperation. Together, the three of them formed a new household of patriots on the Turkish Riviera and they lived happily ever after.

Abdullah and I prepared our reports together-- that's why they seemed so similar. It took some imagination, but we were able to concoct a product that would be acceptable to all and let the newspapers describe the affair as "closed."

"Major Orwell's body was laid to rest with honors at the Incirlik air base in Turkey where he served as Commander. He died while in the service of his country. The two suspects, believed to be of Turkish origin, could have poisoned him while they were playing cards together. The suspects were apprehended and questioned. The Turkish Federal Prosecutor's office announced that there was insufficient evidence to justify bringing the case to trial."

The suspects have not been seen since. There are rumors that they were exiled to an unnamed country. Other rumors have circulated that their own people may have killed them to keep hidden the secret nature of the crime.

THE PREACHERS

BY THE time I arrived at my office the "suits" in Washington and Langley were leaving daily messages for me to report back. What the hell did they think I was doing? Did they suppose I had nothing to do but play their administrative games? Their messages advised me of an upcoming, joint meeting of CIA and State Department representatives. I would be one of the presenters and the topic would be, "Why Our Intelligence on Iraq Failed So Badly."

That's the thanks I got for doing my job! I had been out there on the line of fire in Iraq and I was furious that the "suits" were trying to blame me for the lack of information about Iraq. They seemed to think I should have given them a weekly printed program in advance of events. Did they expect precise entries such as-- "On July 14, 1958 at 8:00 A.M. army tanks will fire on the Royal Palace and kill the king?"

They could just wait for me to get to the conference venue; it served them right. I took care of a few matters in the office during the next few days.

They put on their long faces when I entered the conference room (my execution chamber). By that time I couldn't care less if they fired me; I sort of wished they would. They asked me to summarize the political situation in Iraq, but add my own observations and opinions.

My presentation took almost an hour. I made my points so well that the tenor of the meeting changed from crucifying me to begging me to help them improve the existing intelligence system in Iraq.

We discussed moving the central base of operations from Baghdad to the northern city of Kirkuk. About the only other suggestion I could make for improving the intelligence gathering was to speed up projects already in place.

A year ago a large grant had been made from secret funds to a non-profit organization captained by a Washington operative. He assembled some rag-tag evangelical bible-thumpers who were unemployed. Within a year a dozen of them were ready to go to the Middle East on assignment and keep their eyes and ears open. They were under my command and reported to the CIA office in Istanbul.

Two groups were formed to go to Iraq with three "brothers" in each. One group of three went to the northern city of Kirkuk and the other three to Basra in the south. Each group would be like an advance-warning unit. Like a military unit, they would stay alert to any advances of the Arab Nationalist enemy.

The retired missionary trained them in the Washington area. During his missionary work abroad he had been on our payroll. We hired him again because he knew the tricks of the trade. He worked closely with the 12 recruits both in persuasive Bible promotion and in the fundamentals of "Information Services."

Al these recruits were born-again Christians and eager to spread God's word according to the scriptures. They were devoted to their cover activities because they believed they were in Iraq to rescue Christianity from the Infidel. Things hadn't changed all that much since the days of the Crusades. They were indoctrinated to believe sincerely that America needed to save the Christian world.

They knew how much they were needed because we sent them into areas where they would find desolate minorities of co-religionists eager to collaborate. In the north they were embedded into the ancient Chaldean Christian community. The southern group infiltrated the pre-Christian marshland dwellers, who followed John the Baptist's teachings.

Both local groups were similar to the garden-variety Arab community but each minority had its own history dating back to the time of Jesus. They readily accepted outside support because they found it hard to hold their own in the foreign sea of Muslims. Both societies were an interesting people who always had been marginalized from the mainstream of Muslim Arabs. They were aliens in their own country.

The Iraqi government usually was reluctant to persecute preachers for proselytizing. That gave us good protection for the espionage aspect of our work.

Our preachers enjoyed their assignments very much. They welcomed the opportunity to serve Christ and expand the basis for their own faith through a broader understanding. We in turn, started receiving all sorts of information about those Iraqis that had been ignored and minimized because they were outside the religious mainstream. These outsiders were potential collaborators for promoting our goals.

So there I was, running a Sunday School in the outback regions of Iraq! No matter how much you knew about the Middle East you could always learn more. We made just one stupid miscalculation. Fate dealt itself a hand in the game.

We didn't think it was practical to expect one single preacher to develop enough of a foothold to operate our project. He would need the support of at least one other brother of similar thinking. For extra security we added a third brother. That would give them a small "crowd" to fall back on in adversity. One missionary might be killed but assassinating all three would be too outrageous.

Our initial plan employed the idea of maintaining a threesome in each of the groups, and was based in the tradition about marriages.

One lone wife has too much to deal with and the life is too lonely. Two might develop insoluble disputes-- one against the other. Three in a unit provides for an alliance of two with the third one left with an independent voice.

There was the unrecognized assumption underlying our planning that all three members of the group would support each other. We learned that a group of three spies wouldn't work together any better than would three wives.

Levi was the weak link in our chain. His name suggested that he was Jewish but only because it was the name of an Old Testament prophet. He was a staunch Christian, or appeared to be until he widened his Biblical horizons by living in Iraq.

He always had followed the lessons in the Scripture blindly. Acquiring the perspective of ancient history made him realized that the Scriptures, and the teachings of Jesus, were for a particular period. They could well prove irrelevant at a later time or to a non-Christian society.

As he saw deficiencies in his former beliefs he learned new perspectives in Islam that were never envisioned in his orthodox Christian life.

Although the three brothers-in-faith enthusiastically supported their basic belief in God they became estranged. They could not agree on the religious dogma. Their evening discussions were aimed at reconverting Levi and strengthening their own beliefs.

Levi's independent thinking threatened their essential dogma. The incriminations became harder to bear and they drank more and more araq liquor to ease the pain occasioned by Levi's apostasy. From a "Band of the Faithful" they turned into mean, bitter preachers.

They went on suffering these doctrinal quarrels; recriminations took over their lives. That all changed when Levi disappeared.

Levi failed to return to his bed one night with no warning. Lord knows he had enough reason to avoid his quarrelsome companions, but he had never stayed away before. The next day brought no news. Levi was missing; nobody in town saw him.

When a spy goes missing it is a serious matter. When a missionary spy disappears everybody becomes doubly concerned. The following day his companions officially acknowledged his absence by contacting me in Istanbul.

I tried to minimize public awareness of Levi's absence because I always want to keep my employer out of the picture. We didn't want agents to be spectacles or heroes-- our first aim always was to continue to operate unnoticed. I was on the first flight I could get to Baghdad. None of the six implanted missionaries had been exposed as spies yet, and we needed to keep it that way.

We were losing our grip now that the Iraqi Republic had been established. Suddenly we found ourselves dealing only with enemies. Our friends in the government lay long buried. If we weren't careful our missionary agents would join them. It was becoming very important not to remind the citizens of our presence in their country.

Shortly after I arrived my agents briefed me on the suspected abduction of Levi. The two remaining missionaries were very upset and wanted to help but there was not much to be done. I tried to keep my cool and gather all the information that might help in our search. The two brothers became quite agitated as they related to me the changes in Levi that took place since I last saw him.

Living just a short while in the non-Christian world had corrupted Levi by widening his spiritual horizons. He was no longer one of the Ministers of the Gospel like his two brothers.

They, in their turn, admitted that they viewed Levi as a heretic and they acted as if they were searching around for the nearest stone to pelt him with. "Levi went away in a huff and that was the last we saw of him." A week passed and they had neither seen nor heard from him. Levi was missing and nobody in town had seen him, either.

I praised the two remaining agents for having been wise enough to be discrete about the matter. I sent an alert to all of our agents within a 500-mile radius, but no news of our missing agent came back in the next few days.

I sympathized with my men because they were living monastic lives. I said, "I realize that you can't find a women here to satisfy your needs. You can't even find a Playgirl magazine to entertain yourselves."

One of them was very embarrassed but said that Levi had a close friend from town. This friend would come to the house so that he and Levi could go for walks. He was a nice boy but was always hugging and kissing like a woman. It reached the point where Levi's behavior with the boy embarrassed the others.

They said that they had learned from villagers that Levi's boyfriend was a bum boy They said he actually obliged some of the men in the village for money. They tried to cover their embarrassment by declaring that they really didn't know if Levi and the boy did anything wrong together. Then they contradicted themselves by suggesting that Levi and the boy might have had a lover's quarrel and the boy might have killed Levi.

I sent them to town to bring back the boy. When he arrived I asked to see him alone. He admitted that he had performed sexual acts with Levi but declared with tears in his eyes that he would never have hurt him. He said he was in love with Levi-- I believed him.

It was time to expand my search. I had an informant working undercover among the followers of John the Baptist. I arranged a meet with him and apprised him of the situation. After two days we met again, but he had nothing much to report. He said that one of his friends noticed the two other missionaries down at the bank of the river late one night a week ago.

He arranged for me to interview that witness. I learned that the missionaries seldom went out late at night but they did so that one time. They seemed to be carrying something heavy and they sneaked about suspiciously.

I went back to the house and told the two remaining brothers that I knew what had happened. I didn't know anything at all, but I hoped to trick them. After all, spies are not obliged to tell the truth.

I told them, "One of the fishermen found a dead body about five miles down-stream. They wondered if it might be one of the preachers in our camp because the corpse had light-colored skin."

They appeared surprised and asked about the condition of the body. I told them that I hadn't inquired. They jumped too quickly at the chance to exonerate themselves, "It couldn't have been Levi if the corpse was found only five miles away." They hemmed and hawed, but finally broke down and told me what really had happened.

They made a shocking revelation. They said that one night Levi stood boldly before them in ultimate defiance. He pronounced the Muslim Profession of Faith: "God is Great! God is Great! God is Great! I bear witness that there is no god except *the God,* and Mohammed is his messenger."

They realized that Levi had not only accepted Islam, but also denounced his Christian beliefs when he made the Declaration. The araq they drank had not dulled their minds sufficiently for them to be able to accept this apostasy. They both threw themselves on him and beat him and tore off his clothes. Some dark ancestral memory took over and they were compelled to silence this heretic as was done in the old days. Killing him was the proper thing to do.

They were immobilized with horror over what they had done. They sat unable to speak, with the corpse before them. They desperately drank themselves into insensibility. The liquor postponed the recollection of their descent into madness until the next morning.

They were holy men but still they were human. If they could hide the body they might never be called upon to pay for their crime. They put avoidance of punishment first; they could worry about atonement later.

They stripped off his clothes and took him to the kitchen. There they decapitated him and cut off his hands at the wrists to make identification more difficult. They decided to take him to the river for a final baptism as the only honorable gesture they could make.

They delivered him to the fishes and fed his clothes to a fire. They scoured the reception room and the kitchen and then informed the police about their missing colleague. Then they sat back and waited for the community to spawn speculations and rumors.

They preferred to leave their own judgment until The Day of Resurrection. They hoped that they had the protection of God. They would learn if God was Christian or Muslim.

I was in a quandary about what to do. I couldn't make a big fuss with the police without exposing our espionage operations there. Maybe I should have executed both of them myself but I'm not moralist enough to require justice. Besides I would have had to dispose of two bodies.

It didn't take me long to realize that doing nothing was best, and that it really was all I could do. I took steps to close down that spy operation completely.

The political instability that developed after the revolution had made our whole operation no longer viable. I didn't waste any time looking for Levi's body. I wouldn't have known what to do with it if I'd found it.

CULTURAL WEAPONS

The sneaky French felt that they had been dealt out of the Middle Eastern game for too long. They responded by enhancing their own insidious infiltration of the Middle East and perversion of the Arabic culture of the Lebanon and North Africa. Over decades they were successful at implanting their language into the schools in Lebanon, Algeria, Tunis, and Morocco. The addition of French and Berber words to the vocabulary, divided the people of North Africa by making the local language unintelligible to Arabs from other regions.

Their colonies proudly imported everything French. National identity with other Arabic-speaking people was discouraged, "If you want to be a part of the new world then you had to behave like a Frenchman, not an Arab." Of course this big push to Frenchify the people pleased the priests. Millions of souls were saved for the glory of Christian France!

The West always has attacked the cultural systems of foreign countries to open them up to foreign manipulation. They want those natives to become Westernised and thereby become dependent upon them. The French vigorously suppressed the use of Arabic in their colonies. Schools were required to teach subject matters in French. They opened up new pastures for evangelical Christians and rewarded the converts from Islam to their true Christian faith.

The American Feminist movement had been losing support for years because society was successfully realizing many of their goals in America. They sought new horizons and alighted on the Muslim world.

American Feminists decided to focus on Morocco since it was geographically closest to the West and had already been softened up by French cultural assaults.

America quietly funded grants to "educators" to go over and promote dissention over the cultural and religious restrictions found in Morocco. America was trying to Christianise the natives and gain political control in this sneaky way. This subtle approach appealed to the French and they coordinated they efforts in Lebanon with the Americans.

The subtlety of the American approach permitted them to conduct their anti-Arab, anti-Islamic activities successfully. At the same time the Americans protected the country's rulers from protest and insurrection. Moroccan women complained to the Western press about how Islam was depriving them of their civil liberties. American intentions were suspect to the rest of the world, but the American women themselves, were delighted that somebody was speaking out.

I was annoyed over the protocol problems that were introduced by having our female Vice President come for a visit to a Muslim monarch. Washington sent her anyway. It seemed like America likes to shove our official representatives up the noses of foreign leaders. Our representatives abroad are viewed as the least diplomatic in the entire world. They always have a chip on the shoulder and feel obliged to display American superiority. We are dedicated to violating their customs in order to assert the correctness of our own ways.

Madam Vice President insisted on bringing her dog with her! Do you see what I mean? Dogs run around and step in all kinds of poop and lick at it too-- they lick other dirty things, too! Then they beg to be petted while they wipe their feet on your person. Middle Easterners, especially Muslims, believe dogs should be kept outside in the yard to guard the house. Our VP became a big nuisance to her hosts when she took her pet on a trip like that. The host will be annoyed, and even insulted. You can be sure that the guests and employees of the hotel were offended by this inconsiderateness.

Our President sent his VP and her dog over in the Air Force One plane. This special treatment for a woman and her creature was less to impress the Moroccans than American women voters. Honoring women could get presidential votes the next time around, but deference to pets only makes him look stupid to the Moroccans.

The schedule was all arranged. The king of Morocco was to meet the American VP (and her dog) as she deplaned. They would go to the royal palace together.

He never showed up! Everyone was so shocked-- this was a gross insult. No one knew what to do. A lesser functionary met her and escorted her to a suite inside the airport. The king still did not appear.

Finally, the confused officials organized a face-saving parade to escort the VP from the airport to the palace. She closeted herself with her Ambassador and made it very clear to him that he was obliged to respond to this insult. The Moroccan government confessed total ignorance as to what went wrong.

Those of us in the know recognized this as a formal snub directed at America's interference with the cultural affairs of a sovereign country-- especially by a woman!

The Ambassador sent for me after he was finally able to get the VP off his back. He asked me if I could suggest some retaliation against the King that would keep him from ending up being the winner. I said,

"Sure!" I didn't have any idea what to do but I had been around enough to know that we would be able to come up with something nasty.

Two American-funded award ceremonies had been scheduled back-to-back to coincide with the VP's visit. The Female Scholar of the Year award was to be made by his Highness on the following day.

The day after that the VP would be presenting the award for "Miss Teenager." Of course, the King would not attend that affair because of the cultural inappropriateness of openly displaying female charms. He already had announced his opposition to such disrespectful contests in his kingdom. There was no way he would sanction such goings on with his presence.

The locals talked French and Arabic and we spoke English. It was easy to miscommunicate. The local arrangers never understood that the Miss Teenager ceremony had replaced the scholastic award ceremony.

The king arrived the next day to award a copy of the Holy Quran to the Scholar of the Year and found himself in the midst of a raging teenager mob. He was besieged by half-naked bodies and roiling charms. He left in a fury and in disgrace. Sometimes the representatives of two cultures shouldn't try to mesh. Another barrier to divide God's children had been buttressed.

BAGMAN

I CLEARED my desk of paperwork and was sitting back wondering what I should do. I could go to the tennis courts and try to find a partner with time on his hands or I could go home and read a book. In my head I vetoed going home and reading because it was too lovely an afternoon to waste indoors.

It turned out that I did neither. I failed to escape a phone call from Langley by sitting in my chair, contemplating these welcome diversions. A CIA administrator from Washington explained that they were depending upon my reliability to carry an important package from Washington to Istanbul. The instructions I received were few.

"Travel under your own name, Adam Chelabi, and register at the Barlow Hotel in Washington. Wait in the hotel room for a courier to bring a package and a name. Guard the package with your life.

Return to your embassy in Istanbul and wait for the Turkish courier named by the American courier. You will then turn over the package to the Turk and accompany him to the embassy exit where he probably will have an escort waiting. That will conclude your mission."

I understood that this was some sort of payoff and so I complied with my instructions to the letter. When the mission was completed, I did what I wasn't supposed to do-- I followed the Turkish courier to see which office he delivered the package to. He went into the Opposition

Party offices and returned to the street empty-handed. It looked like I was the agent chosen to deliver a bribe to "The enemy within." That really was not much of a surprise.

I went back to my office wondering what it was that the Americans wanted from the former president, now present leader of the opposition. Within two days the opposition party was urging their government to allow the American military full access to the Turkish national airbase at Incirlik. This acceptance of a larger American military presence in Turkey would strengthen them against Russia, but might provoke a preemptory response. At the very least the government officials could expect verbal abuse from the political opposition.

Everything was going according to plan and the cold war was being cemented in place. America was developing distant sites for missiles and arms storage, and was opening up advance positions for spying and intercepting Russian messages.

I was very happy to see America standing successfully against Russia. I was less delighted to see America becoming even further entrenched in my beloved Turkey. Formulating policy wasn't any of my business-- I just carried it out. I fulfilled my mission properly and that is what really mattered-- or was it?

Several years would pass before I would be called upon again to be the courier for such a large, secret payment.

* * * * *

America was increasingly successful in building its military operations in Turkey. America controlled the Baghdad Pact, and the Baghdad Pact members controlled Turkey. Compliance with America's wishes produced AID money and lots of arms, but alienated the public. The people felt that they no longer controlled their own country. Underneath it all was the overly powerful Turkish military that formulated the policies that the Turkish politicians espoused.

The military leaders felt secure enough to demand more bribe money. The amount was so large that the State Department looked around for a reliable career employee to serve temporarily as courier. They recalled how effectively I had conveyed their bribe a few years earlier and so they rang me up with the usual instructions. I didn't mind the task. It was much better than a lot of the distasteful jobs I had to perform.

My instructions for delivery were the same. I should secure the money in my office and wait for the Turkish party to contact me for delivery. I came back to Istanbul with the package and the Turkish courier's name.

You may remember that the previous time I followed the courier to the actual recipient of the bribe. I planned to do the same thing again. The more knowledge you have about an operation, the more likely you can be sure that it will work out successfully.

This time I took the additional step of opening the package and examining the contents. No surprise there-- five million dollars in freely negotiable bearer bonds. I tucked them away in my office safe to await pick up.

Then came the shocking news! My secretary came in from the outer office to tell me that the Chief of Staff of the military leadership of the government had been assassinated. It must have happened about the same time that I arrived at the airport with the money. His aide de camp was killed also. They were both shot in the chest, each with a single accurately placed bullet. The ammunition reportedly consisted of government-issued exploding-tip shells. It seemed almost too professional to have been perpetrated by anyone in the military.

I wondered if this killing would have any effect on the bribery deal. There were all sorts of possible ramifications. The military might renege on some of their very permissive arrangements with the Baghdad Pact members. They might threaten to counterbalance the Americans by inviting the Soviets to extend their assistance. I didn't know what to expect so I just figured I'd wait quietly until the courier showed up to claim the bundle.

What actually happened was that the assassination of such a key leader unlocked all sorts of competition for political control and brought out repressive attempts by the army to control it. Istanbul would be in turmoil until the leadership was sorted out.

This disruption of government seems to have been the objective of those citizens behind the assassination. We supposed that the perpetrators of this action were opposed to the sell out of the Incirlik airbase and the misuse of Turkey's military power. They wanted the legislators to have second thoughts about being such acquiescent sheep.

After a few days no one had come to collect the bribe money. It looked like I was the only one in Istanbul, who knew it existed. I figured that the secrecy surrounding such a transaction had prevented political successors from claiming the money.

Time passed and I decided to move the stash from my office safe to my mattress. Nobody came to collect it so I just slept on my treasure and waited. The general didn't need it where he went. Each day I became fonder of my lumpy mattress. I was thinking of the stash as my retirement fund.

The five million wouldn't do me any good while I was a CIA employee. I started wondering what I could do with my fortune if I were free of my employer.

We used to joke about taking early retirement from the CIA-- "You don't retire from the CIA, you just retire from seeing the green side of the turf to staring at the brown roots."

I lived with these uncertainties for about a week. I figured Washington either didn't know what was going on or couldn't decide to whom they should redirect the bribe money. I kept expecting to get instructions from Langley telling me what to do with it.

The week passed by and those instructions never came. I realized that nobody except me knew what had happened to the money. The few people involved only knew about their own part in the process. Each completed his task and assumed that the matter was finished.

I HAD FOUND A FIVE MILLION DOLLAR RETIREMENT FUND!

I had been Regional Head of CIA for almost five years. I was 49 years old and felt that I had wasted my life. I wanted to quit and go spend the rest of my life working in my father's new, five-star hotel in Istanbul.

When you were a kid did you ever jump into a lake and find yourself surrounded by slithering eels? That's the way I felt about working in the Middle East those days. I could no longer justify doing my job. I was becoming absolutely disgusted with everything America did in the Middle East. Zionism and Imperialism replaced the so-called Christian values of gentility and brotherly love.

CYPRUS

WHILE nothing developed with respect to the money, it was a different story in the law enforcement area. All the police were on watch for information about the sniper who killed the Chief of Staff. All confidential informers had all been alerted to look for leads to those who planned the killing behind the scenes.

As soon as Abdullah's division came up with a lead he asked me to meet him to share what information he had. The perpetrators didn't appear to be involved in anything that would be of direct concern to the CIA. It was just that Abdullah wanted to share with me that which everybody in the country was talking about, although the public had little information.

He told me that the police had dependable information that the sniper had flown from Istanbul to Turkish Cyprus a day earlier. There were certainly enough patriots hiding out in Turkish Cyprus to make it almost impossible to discover his precise location.

Abdullah said, "We haven't done anything interesting together for almost a year. Do you think you can justify the pursuit of this fugitive as part of your job? If not, maybe you could just take vacation time and go with me to Cyprus?"

I thought about it for almost a whole minute. I told him, "You've got a deal!" The next day we met at the boarding gate of the Istanbul airport. We were a little early so I suggested a raku to kill some time. We talked excitedly about what we would do on our first night out together in almost a year. Abdullah knew the island better than I since I had only been there just for business conferences. He used to go there on holidays with his parents

Cypress was the nub or nexus of all major spy operations in the world. Regardless of your credentials, you entered Cyprus as a master spy even though you may have been only a low-status courier or a tourist. Every foreigner was assumed to be a spy and was treated respectfully.

Cyprus is a fun place even though this lovely island is separated by bitterness into a Greek section and a Turkish one. Travel between the two sections was very restricted and required armed convoys to travel along the highways between cities in the different sections. Anyhow, that was no problem. We were Turks and had passports that said so. We had no more reason to bother with the Greeks, than they with us.

The Cyprus police met us at the airport and they escorted us through immigration and customs without any checks. That was just as well because I decided at the last minute to bring along the purloined $5,000.000 in bearer bonds.

The police took us to the barracks to check us into our sleeping quarters in the Bachelor Officers' Quarters. I asked Abdullah what we would do about transportation in the evening. He arranged to have a car and plainclothes driver meet us at the quarters at nine P.M.

We had a few drinks in the Bachelor Officers' Club and visited with some of the guys stationed there. They asked about our mission. We told them the truth, "We're here to arrest the citizen who shot the General." They told us that the shooting made quite a splash among the army officers. Their own sympathy seemed to lie with the assassin; they were suggesting that the General had become too big for his britches. They opined that it would be hard to capture the perpetrator with the small amount of cooperation we could count on.

Then we tested the water. We confessed that we were not very determined to complete our mission successfully. We admitted that some brave citizen had done the country a lot of good by pulling the trigger. One of the guys asked us, "What will you do with the assassin if you catch him." I said, "We'll question him if we take him alive. We will force him to tell us the names of the conspirators behind his actions."

The challenger continued, "And after you get the names what will you do?" I replied, "We probably will turn him loose if his backers are people we know and approve of. If they are connected with Turkey's foreign enemies we probably will shoot him and then go back to Turkey and arrest his co-conspirators."

Then the challenger upped the ante-- "And what if we were protecting him; what would you do?" "Probably go back to Istanbul empty-handed after being entertained by you guys." I asked him outright, "Are you saying that we might be able to reach an agreement that would leave everybody happy?" He smiled and said, "Why don't you guys go out tonight and have some fun. We'll talk about this again tomorrow evening, OK?"

Only then did he introduce himself, "My name is Mehmet," and he smiled and reached out to grasp my hand. "We'll see you here tomorrow night and maybe we can work something out." When we left Mehmet we were optimistic that our mission would go well.

It was just too easy. Abdullah agreed that everything was going too well. I said, "To hell with it! Let's just have fun tonight." We passed the best hotel in the Turkish sector and I told the driver to pull over. I got out and went to reception and paid for a two-bed room for two nights. Abdullah protested that it was too expensive. Then I told him, "I'm damned if I'm going to sleep in a camp using five million dollars as a pillow for my head.

He was properly shocked. We sat down, or should I say, "collapsed" in the lounge. That's when I told him...

"I stole five million dollars for my retirement fund and now I'm on the run! I didn't exactly steal the money; I just modified a pay-off so that it went to me instead of to a treasonous political leader. I have known for some time that I could not keep on doing the things demanded of me by the CIA. My country always seems to be on the side of evil and I could no longer serve her.

This bribe money we were paying to the Turkish General Chief of Staff was in my safe and I was the only person, who knew it still existed. Everybody assumed that the payoff had been completed before the General was assassinated and I didn't have to do anything except wait. After a week I decided to disappear in such a manner that everybody would assume that I was dead. Your invitation to join you on this mission provided me the opportunity that I needed to escape."

I outlined my plan to Abdullah and asked if he would help me stage my phony death. He agreed reluctantly to assist. We talked about how it might be accomplished. As we talked he became excited and enthusiastic. Finally, he admitted, "Yes! It's a good plan. It's so good I'm tempted to go with you. I no longer feel that the leaders of my country are working for the people's benefit and I wish I could get out, too!"

My response was, "We've got five million dollars which is enough for both of us to start new lives far from the wrath of our employers. Half of what I have is yours."

He admitted that he was tempted. As for me, I would be delighted to have my best friend accompany me in breaking away. When I made the final separation it would be forever; I knew it would be very lonely without family. It would be worth two and a half million to know that he would always be at my side.

We had a few more drinks and then agreed to sleep on it before taking irreversible steps. We invited a couple of bar girls to join us and we celebrated our secret pact like a couple of criminal conspirators. The night passed by too quickly.

I was asking Abdullah to give up all connections with his family forever-- that would not be easy for him to do. I was afraid he would decide in the morning that he was either not brave enough or not evil enough to proceed with the plan.

Back in the hotel we tossed in our beds. We were either teetering on the brink of success or disaster-- we knew not which. Our plans stood the examination by daylight and we ate a pleasant breakfast together. There was nothing for us to do until we met with Mehmet in the evening.

It seemed like the clock had stopped. One of the hardest parts of the escape procedure proved to be the waiting for Mehmet. He was at the barracks when we arrived; we shook hands amiably. Then I told him as much as he needed to know, "We are quite ready to deliberately fail in our assignment to catch the assassin. All we ask in return from you is to help us deceive our employers by faking our deaths."

I told Mehmet that we would not only help him save the life of the assassin, but would give him ten thousand dollars to split up among the gang just as he pleased. In turn, they would dress Abdullah and me in Greek uniforms to make it look as though we had disguised ourselves to spy on the Greeks. Then they would tie us each to a tree and take photos of our limp bodies smeared with catsup, with eyes closed.

They would report finding the photos and passports in a Greek military jeep. They would say that the jeep must have stalled because of some engine trouble. They would report that they failed to find any trace of the two bodies. It would be supposed that the two men were shot by the Greeks and buried out in no-man's land. We agreed to meet Mehmet in three days. That period should prove sufficient to make final arrangements.

The most difficult part of the plan was to get Abdullah's agreement to give up his family and his old life. He admitted that his good life made it hard for him to make the final break. We provisioned ourselves with Lebanese passports that would substantiate our new status in life.

We met Mehmet as planned and he gave us the Greek uniforms. I asked him where they got them. He said, "There is always some Greek soldier dying, who can provide a uniform. If not, then we take a prisoner about to be released and strip him down to his underwear and repatriate him in his embarrassing condition." We agreed to stage our execution for midmorning of the next day.

After the photos were taken we gave them and our old passports to Mehmet to report having found them in the Jeep at the side of the road. We finally reached the point where there was no turning back. I cashed out my smallest denomination bond so that we would have traveling money. Then we obtained tickets for a boat leaving the next morning for the Syrian port of Latakia.

Both of us had long faces as we boarded the overnight ferry to Latakia. We both knew that stepping from the shore onto the gangplank was the hardest thing we would ever have to do. Maybe it was a mistake? Who knows until the hand is played out? Could we still change our minds? No, it was too late.

If you watch TV dramas about spies then you will believe that it is impossible to opt out on your master. That is mostly fiction. Your former boss just wants to be sure that you don't reveal any secrets to the enemy. He doesn't expect you to go around blabbing but he knows that money, liquor, and torture can quickly loosen the tongue.

You can stay hidden if you follow a few precautions. If your boss searches fruitlessly for you then he will be assured that the other side won't find you either. Then you will be free, except for the persistent habit of looking over your shoulder.

All you need to do is follow the three rules: Get out of Dodge; Dump every personal possession-- even your pen; and last, Change your hirsute appearance. Even your mother won't recognize you in a strange country when you are wearing a beard or mustache instead of being clean-shaven. Mehmet had our old telltale passports and may have turned them over to his chief already.

We had faced difficult decisions before but that didn't make it any easier to go ahead with this one. We flashed a brave smile at each other. We knew what the other was thinking and feeling-- we had that kind of brotherly relationship.

What should have been a pleasant boat cruise became a misery as we reflected on what we had done. When we left the families behind it was like we had died-- or was it more like they died and left us alone? Would we ever again build a happy life or would we be fugitives whose only pleasure is avoiding the authorities for just one more day?

The passage was slow-- or so it seemed. We were about to go through the next to the last checkpoint before settling down to a quiet life. We cleared immigration and customs without any problems.

Our spirits rose as we stepped out into Syria, our first rescue point after leaving Turkish-controlled areas. We ate the best meal we had in days at a small restaurant on the waterfront. Syrian food is generally very delicious. We were in no hurry so we drank a few brandies to top it off.

We checked into a hotel to spend the night before starting out on our next day's trek to Lebanon. It was safer to split up our wealth so I gave half of my bonds to Abdullah.

We left no trail for our employers to follow. We avoided passing through the coastal towns and cities by traveling along the smaller roads that hugged the foothills of the mountains that paralleled the Mediterranean coast. We used busses and collective taxis to move from one destination to another. There were no tickets to betray our path.

We had overcome most of the obstacles to our escape. I knew I would feel better once we crossed over into Lebanon. For the first time since we started the journey we met with a challenge. The guard at the crossing into Lebanon opened our luggage and found the bonds. He wanted to know what "these papers" were.

He was at a loss because he could only read Arabic characters, not Latin ones. I told him, "These are graduation diplomas for our students in the English-supported school we work for. We are taking them to Beirut but want to stop and visit in the mountains while on our way." He grunted and closed our luggage. We, in turn, started breathing again.

MEANWHILE

THE big, black Limousine pulled up in front of Father's new luxury hotel in the Sultan Ahmet district of Istanbul. The car flew the American flags; this was no casual visitor. The companion to the chauffeur, who appeared to be American, moved slowly and quietly like a cat. He announced the arrival of the American Ambassador to the doorman and was invited inside. After a few minutes he came out and went over to the limousine to talk with the occupant.

He explained that the area seemed secure and that Mr. Chelabi was expecting him. Another bodyguard accompanied the Ambassador as he climbed out of the car and the three approached the hotel. All hell broke loose two minutes after they went inside. A man, screaming like a woman, shattered the quietness of the morning and the noise from inside the hotel rose to become thunder.

The staff had grabbed Father to keep him from collapsing and hurting himself. Poor Father! The ambassador had just told him that I was dead-- that I was killed in the line of duty in Cyprus. All who tried to comfort him burst into tears themselves. At times like that there is nothing anyone can do to help. The ambassador stood quietly at his side.

Father demanded answers as he recovered a little-- he wanted to know how it had happened. The ambassador choked out the little information he had. After expressing his sympathy he explained:

"Your son went to Cyprus with his friend Abdullah from the International branch of the Istanbul Police. They went to arrest the assassin of the Turkish Chief of Staff. Together, they chased him from Istanbul to the Turkish territory in Cyprus.

They located him with the help of some Turkish informers and tried to arrest him and return him to Istanbul. Either they failed to hire enough help to make the arrest or they were betrayed. Both Adam and Abdullah were overcome and disarmed when the assassin's friends rescued him.

Adam and Abdullah couldn't be taken back to the Turkish base; they were hidden in an old Turkish army camp near the place they had been captured. This camp was little used by the Turks because it was so close to the Greek border that it was a liability.

A rogue Greek army squad must have attacked the camp before our two men could be moved to a more secure location. The Turkish renegades were able to retreat successfully but left our men behind in shackles. Our two heroes were each tied to a tree and summarily tried for spying. They were found guilty and so it was a simple matter to carry out the execution order.

The Greek squad took photos of the bodies tied to the trees to provide evidence of the fate of the two "spies." They demanded $10,000 for the photos. I knew how upset you would be so I made copies of the photos so you could look at them later when you felt able. I will leave them here on the table. For now you have enough to deal with. We have offered another $10,000.00 for information leading us to a recovery of the bodies.

There have been no takers so we believe that either the bodies were buried secretly or else destroyed. The Greek army made a superficial inquiry but only produced a two-page report setting forth some of what I am telling you now.

They knew of no renegade squad and concluded that the whole matter was just a made-up hoax to make trouble for the Greeks. They denied that any of it had ever actually happened."

That's the picture the ambassador had. The truth differed in one important respect-- we were alive and well!

SHUF MOUNTAINS

IT was slow going but we finally reached the foothills of the Shuf Mountains of Lebanon where an old friend lived. We took our places in a rickety bus that agonized its way up the mountain. We arrived at my friend Raouf's village. I had not seen him for several years and friends in our kind of work have the bad habit of disappearing-- dying or being imprisoned. I knew we would be welcome if he was OK.

We left the bus and walked to Raouf's home just on the edge of the village. Our luck held; he was at home and was delighted to see me. We had arrived too late for the noon meal so Raouf presented us with araq and *mezza* (finger-food) and promised to feed us properly on the next day so the women would have time to prepare food.

I stretched back out on the large, soft bolsters and cushions of Raouf's parlor. I wallowed in the realization that our escape was over. We had made our break successfully and could start our new lives without the fears that nag fugitives.

We spent the first two days just visiting; no mention of our escape entered the conversation. After all, we had the rest of our lives to devote to this relocation, why be in a hurry?

Raouf was overjoyed when we explained that we had left Turkey for good, so that we could take up new lives as his countrymen. He praised us and congratulated us, and he swore that this is the best thing that we ever could have done. He promised me his sister in wedlock and he said that he couldn't wait to have me in the family as a brother-in-law. You just can't get a better welcome than that!

The more we discussed our new circumstances, the more I realized that an alliance with his family would provide us with legitimacy, should any of our agents check up on our *bona fides*. His friends would become mine once I was accepted into the family. There was only one drawback-- his enemies would become my enemies also.

The Lebanese mountain dwellers had been fighting as far back as history reaches. In the time of the Crusades, the Europeans widened the breaches between communities. They took advantage of minor differences to set one group at their neighbor's throat and then stood around mopping up the spoils.

French adventurers employed that strategy in Lebanon-- "Divide and conquer." Muslims were played against Christians. Shi'i Muslims were used to attack the Sunni Muslims. Raouf's Druze ancestors were encouraged to quarrel with all these other groups.

I had to wonder if I weren't stepping in one pile of dog shit while avoiding another. But retreat was impossible; there was no path leading back. Of course we had regrets even though we knew we were doing the right thing.

Abdullah and I were together all the time. We shared sleeping quarters and we spent our days out walking and visiting neighbors. We sat around talking with Raouf when he was free. We had to be careful not to slip backward and provide trails to our former identities, so we were forced to submerge ourselves fully in our new style of life. The two of us switched from talking together in Turkish all the time. We needed to improve our Arabic to match our new nationality.

Within a month the idleness was beginning to get old. Abdullah and I agreed that we should get on with our new lives. We discussed the advisability of creating new families vs. continuing on with our selfish concerns and then establish families later-- perhaps never.

It was tempting to take a wife from the village. She could provide some badly needed companionship in our lonely, selfish lives. There was a shortage of eligible males in the village as in most other parts of the mountains. Bachelors and husbands alike had been decimated by the inter-tribal warfare. Many widows spent the winters alone in cold beds, huddling with their orphans.

Both Abdullah and I were in our late forties so we had good reason not to postpone establishing families much longer. We had plenty of choices because widows with young children were eager to re-establish homes. The community would be particularly pleased if we selected mates with children. Widows belong to the community and must be cared for. Their orphans belong to everybody so all adults are parents in *loco parentis.*

Raouf's sister was a very attractive widow in her early 30's and she had three children aged five through ten. Her husband had been killed in a roadside skirmish on a disputed path when the enemy village decided to use rifles to demonstrate their lordship over it. Raouf had already spoken to his sister before he approached me seriously.

Raouf plain-out asked me if I wouldn't marry his sister Sa'dia and become a father to her children. He said that they would be so pleased with the arrangement that the family would forego the usual dowry bride-price. I thanked him a hundred times for his affection and kind offer. The more raku I drank the better the arrangement sounded. I consulted Abdullah to help bring closure to the matter. We three got stinko and when I awoke the next day I found myself affianced. All that remained was to complete the marriage formalities.

I started on this adventure with Abdullah and wanted to make sure we would continue down the same road together. I pinned him to the divan cushion as if he were a butterfly in a showcase and then Raouf and I refused to release him until he agreed to marry. We wanted to have a double wedding.

We Middle Easterners are quite practical about matrimonial affairs. Abdullah and I were aware that it would be more important for our two wives to be companionable with each other than to be attracted to the new husband. So we asked Raouf which widow in the village was dearest to his sister Sa'dia. He said that he would ask her. Now that she was promised to me she came under my protection, so we were allowed to sit together and consult.

Sa'dia came into our room and made a few gestures of a housewife tidying up and then alighted in our midst. She brought chi with her and we began our consultation. She exclaimed with delight how happy she would be to have someone from among her friends become her sister-in-law. It gave an unusual and amusing twist to the traditional selection of a bride-- this time a woman chose the bride!

We narrowed her widow friends down to two of her cousins. They were both beloved and she swore that she would be equally happy with either of them. They were sisters with only two years difference in age. One was 23 and the other 25-- with two and three children, respectively. Raouf requested that Sa'dia go to their house and invite them to meet their guests. This was very forward but it was time we stopped dithering and moved along into action. Hell! Everything about this marriage brokering was weird!

The widows arrived after an hour and they stood blushing. I invited them to sit beside us but they were too embarrassed. Only Raouf could persuade them to be seated. What was said was not important. The mutual assessment of one another is what it was all about. After half an hour all three girls withdrew.

Raouf and I both turned to our butterfly and twisted the pin a bit. Abdullah admitted that both prospects would appear to be excellent choices. He declared that he would chose on the basis of doing the greatest good-- age would be the deciding factor. The older girl had three children and therefore had the poorer prospects for recovering a complete family life. Abdullah elected to marry her so that she and her children would live happily ever after.

Raouf left to confer with Sa'dia privately. Five minutes later he returned to our parlor and announced that it was a done deal. I congratulated Raouf on being able to bring about the engagement in a single hour what would have taken the women of the family many weeks.

The families gave an engagement party for the girls. The whole village was the venue and it continued on, right through three consecutive nights. Our fiancées were having the time of their lives. We planned to spend another month in the mountains to give them time to say good-bye and assemble their wedding trousseaus. Besides, we needed a little more time ourselves so that we could adjust to the idea of becoming both husbands and stepfathers.

We descended from the mountains to the nearest Lebanese city in search of a used panel truck and a large open-bodied one. We would need to transport our new families and their goods to Beirut. Raouf and his mother accompanied the four of us as chaperones.

The ladies spent some pleasant hours viewing offerings in several better jewelry stores. On our last day we went to the stores and purchased those things that pleased them most. Abdullah and I both purchased new clothes for the upcoming occasion. All that remained was to exchange final vows.

While we were gone the rest of the ladies back in the village planned the wedding reception for the two marriages. The scheduled time arrived and we all went to the big reception room in Raouf's house.

A sheet was hung between the brides and the witnesses to screen the two brides when they were taking their vows. That way the girls were not subject to so much embarrassment when they were obliged to announce their immodest decision to accept a man in their beds.

Finally the day of departure arrived-- the day we all dreaded. Somehow we managed to get on the road, headed for Beirut, despite all the lamentations and drawn-out good-byes. We made the interior of the panel truck comfortable with carpets and pillows. The rest of our goods went in the back of the larger truck. We two men got behind the wheel with our wives at our side, and we were off.

We spent one night in the trucks and arrived in Beirut in time to settle in for the next night. We found a caravanserai that suited our needs for a temporary refuge. Those stopover places were designed for traders so they are found near the marketplaces. There, a visitor can find a place to coral his animals, store his goods safely, and have a place to sleep at night. The facility was just like it used to be centuries ago except that trucks were replacing the wagon carts, and the beasts that pulled them were no more. The caravanserai is a sort of cross between a campground, and a motel for trucks.

The caravanserai that we stopped at served our purposes very well. In the morning we left the women to their own affairs and went down into the city to search for two rental houses located near one another. We considered which would be the best area for relocating our families. Money was no concern but security was a big one. We could afford to settle in the better part of the city and wanted to live conveniently close to the stores, schools, and attractions, but we had to be wary.

People in the country aren't as critical as the city dwellers; they aren't as nosey. City dwellers are less trusting and want to know too much about you before they accept you. They need to know and understand you to become your friend-- that was exactly what we didn't need. But once you are a neighbor in a rural area you will have the mutual affection and protection that neighbors are due.

Our wives didn't know the facts behind our escape from our employers. They only knew that we were on the run and that anonymity was of utmost importance. We knew that they would understand if we selected a safer location a little outside of the city, even though it might be a bit inconvenient.

We went out each day in the panel truck searching for the right place to settle our families. We found several houses located close to one another but took our time to consider which place would suit us best.

Our wives were anxious to get started on making our new homes, so they urged us to make a decision and get on with life. Abdullah and I were in agreement so we completed the papers to lease two adjacent houses for a five-year period. The two houses belonged to the same owner.

The next day we brought all our things from the caravanserai to our new homes. Only a few steps separated the houses, yet there was enough space for gardens and play yards. The children had plenty of room to romp about under the fruit trees that separated the houses. Everybody was happy.

We had covered our tracks like professionals so we felt reasonably secure. Our wives realized that none of us would ever be able to speak openly about our pasts. The wives and older children had been briefed on what family information they could convey to others-- most of it fabricated.

We were to use the deceased husband's families when describing our origins. We were from their village and we pretended that we had all known each other when the girls were still infants. We were to take over the identity of the natural fathers and must never be described as stepfathers. Our children were told never to discuss their father's business and to never answer questions about him.

My new life was perfect; unfortunately I was not. I had lived so long as a spy that I had developed a suspicious nature and was too controlling-- I trusted no one.

My wife devoted herself completely to our new family and she placed everyone's needs above her own. I gave her as much support and love as I was capable of giving, but she deserved more. She was not unhappy but I felt guilty for being unable to be a better husband and father.

ABRACADABRA

OUR lives were becoming routine and boring after three months of settling in. We missed the excitement of the chase that we used to have in our espionage jobs. Now everything was the same, day after day, and quite predictable. Neither of us had the slightest reservation about the wisdom of having taken early retirement. Both of us enjoyed the youthful animation of our young children and a companionable wife, and we were grateful that we had plenty of free time to spend with them. Needless to say, these were gratifications that we had lacked for a long time.

After we got settled Abdullah and I found it easier to get away from the duties that used to keep us at home, We started going down to the *Hamraa* district of Beirut and hanging out at the cafes there until it was time to return home for the midday meal. We had too much idle time.

We started to look around at business opportunities in the district. At first our interest in the business opportunities was a simple pastime; we were retired and had no need to earn money. Gradually we found that our interests in business possibilities were changing into actual business planning-- idle schemes were morphing into business plans.

I started the snowball rolling from the moment I mentioned Father's success with his Abracadabra take away stores. Those were the international fast-food franchises that made Father a multimillionaire.

The word abracadabra comes from the book "Arabian Nights Entertainment." When Ali Baba pronounced the magic word "Abracadabra" along with "Open Sesame," a gash appeared in the mountain to expose a fabulous treasure.

Within a week we had convinced ourselves that what Beirut needed was another café and restaurant that specialized in kebab (skewer-roasted meat) and falafel (fried bean cakes). After another month we believed that we were destined in life to open such a place. There is no sense arguing with destiny.

Within six months we were sitting in our own café hawking falafel and kebab to the passers-by. On our opening day we said a little prayer to give our thanks to God. Out of earshot of visitors I also gave thanks to God for saving this spy from a miserable "retirement" like Dasher's.

* * * * *

They say that, "The first five years are the hardest." Whatever critical information I used to have locked away in my brain had drifted away into the unimportant past. Even if the enemy found me there would be nothing currently worth extracting from me. With this much passing of time I even could get away with writing and publishing a book like this one, about my adventures as a super spy.

Abdullah and I are solid businessmen of the community. Both our families spend a lot of time together. The ladies take turns preparing dinner and that makes everybody happy. Each wife gets a day off from cooking when the other is preparing the food. Each husband is delighted to have the variety in his diet that is provided by having two excellent cooks prepare his meals.

We spend so much time in each other's house that the children don't differentiate between mother and aunt. When one of the kids has a runny nose he turns to the nearest mother or aunt to wipe it. When a boy stumbles and needs a hug he doesn't seek out his own father, he turns to the man closest to him.

The children are growing up too fast. Soon they will have their own families. Abdullah and I will no longer be what we once were, but we will remember our adventures together. We will relate them to the children and they will smile at us. They will know that we must be making up the stories. Things like that couldn't have happened to two old geezers like us.

* * * * *

Some day one of you may wander into my shop and recognize me. You probably will see my partner Abdullah, too. He will be the amiable fellow playing backgammon with a customer.

I beg you to pass us by and enjoy the kebab from our neighbor's stand. Let us live out our years as brothers of all mankind and enemy of none. May God extend your life for your kindness!

God is Great!

THE END

But a year latter Adam and Abdullah *were* recognized by
Jonathan P. Slow and his friend Wilson.
Learn what happened to all of them in the sequel:

Jonathan Padraig Slow, Exposed.
2014, Amazon

MUSINGS BY YOUR AUTHOR

A STRANGER
My wife says I'm a stranger.
I get stranger every day.

GOOD PEOPLE
Don't you hate it when BAD people do BAD things to
GOOD people?
I hate it even more when GOOD people do GOOD
things to BAD people.

IN AMERICA
The Ultimate mark of success
is to die of cirrhosis of the liver or from an overdose.

AZZA'S CARETAKER
My hope is that Azza's caretaker, Rose, will celebrate
my next wedding with me,
or mourn at my funeral-- whichever comes first.

SOON
One day soon I'm going to step off the edge of the world
and become stardust.

STILL GOT IT
Even if I can't still piss a stream
I still can write books.

GREY CELLS
The old gray mare ain't what she used to be,
neither are the old grey cells.

GOOD SHIT

We all have good shit and bad shit passing through our minds.

The difference between an author and others is that he writes down the good shit.

FAIR

I'm usually considered as being fair with others.
That doesn't mean I'm not prejudiced,
it's only that I'm fair about my prejudices.

AUTHORS

A Good author can write about nothing and make it interesting.

A Bad author can write about something interesting and make it uninteresting.

SUCCESS

Success is less about your luck at drawing cards
than it is about how well you play them.

DECISIONS

Man is a decision-making animal
but most of his decisions are made by his gonads.

MOTHER

My Mother shot me down
with all those pesky diaper changes.
She kept me from being President of the United States.

MIRRORS

When you look in the mirror if you don't see
your best friend, then change mirrors.

DEMOCRACY

America wants democracy in the Middle East and will support whichever *dictator* will give it to the people.

DECISIONS

Life is so full of decisions!
Other people and circumstances usually dictate the decisions taken.
It's rare that we get to make free choices.

ACADEMIA

There are three noteworthy types on university faculties:

The rare scholar who sets unachievably high standards for the others.

The teacher who funnels knowledge into half-interested students, and

The hack who gets by on pleasantries and serves as a target for the enmity of the other types.

PETTINESS

When we grow old our lives are replete with pettiness.

ELIMINATE UNEMPLOYMENT

Make caffeine illegal so we can move users to our jails. Then start another war and draft the remaining unemployed into the army.

AUTHORS

The difference between authors, and preachers and politicians, is that authors disseminate their bullshit sitting down.

AGING

The only advantage to aging is that it absolves you
from all consequences.
There is no future, no tomorrow.
Enjoy today and give thanks.

About the Author

The author is Professor Emeritus in the Florida University System. A Clinical Psychologist by training and a Cultural Anthropologist by interest. He writes under a facetious pseudonym because he wants to keep his personal life separate from his professional one. Finally, after twenty-five years retirement, he elected to write some novels sharing his varied experiences as background.

Nine titles are available from Kindle, Amazon Books, and booksellers around the world. He declares that this will be his last novel, "It's time to *really* retire!" After much pleading he finally agreed to write one last novel, "Jonathan Padraig Slow, Exposed."

He has lived in Baghdad and in Cairo and has made more than 70 trips to Latin America and 15 to Turkey. He is married to a wife from Baghdad and made the pilgrimage to Mecca. His wonderful children still hang out near the nest and encourage him.

Made in the USA
Charleston, SC
22 March 2014